TALES OF A SAD,
FAT WORDMAN

Also by Ralph Dennis

The War Heist
A Talent for Killing
The Broken Fixer
The Spy in a Box
Dust in the Heart

The Hardman Series

Atlanta Deathwatch
The Charleston Knife is Back in Town
The Golden Girl And All
Pimp For The Dead
Down Among The Jocks
Murder Is Not An Odd Job
Working For The Man
The Deadly Cotton Heart
The One Dollar Rip-Off
Hump's First Case
The Last Of The Armageddon Wars
The Buy Back Blues
All Kinds of Ugly

TALES OF A SAD, FAT WORDMAN

RALPH DENNIS

CUTTING EDGE

Copyright © 2020 Adventures in Television, Inc. All Rights Reserved.

"My Friend Hardman" Copyright © 2019 Ben Jones.

"Ralph" Copyright © 2019 Cynthia Williams.

Region of Innocence was originally published in the *Carolina Quarterly,* Vol. 7, issue #3. Spring 1955.

Letter to Kazuko c/o Bar Desire was originally published in the *Carolina Quarterly,* Vol. 12, issue #1. Winter 1959

Excerpts from the Journal of a Sad, Fat Wordman was originally published in *Reflections from Chapel Hill,* Vol 1, Issue #2. July 1961

Return of the Sad, Fat Organization Man was originally published in *Reflections from Chapel Hill.* December 1962

Son of a Sad, Fat Wordman Goes North was originally published in *Lillabulero,* Vol. 1, issue #4. 1967

Wind Sprints was originally published in *Lillabulero,* Vol. 1, issue #2. 1967

The characters and events portrayed in this book are fictitious. Any similarity to real persons, living or dead, is coincidental and not intended by the author.

No part of this book may be reproduced, or stored in a retrieval system, or transmitted in any form or by any means, electronic, mechanical, photocopying, recording, or otherwise, without express written permission of the publisher.

ISBN-13: 978-1-7343480-3-3

Published by
Cutting Edge Publishing, LLC
PO Box 8212
Calabasas, CA 91372

TABLE OF CONTENTS

Introduction by Lee Goldberg · vii

Chapter: 1 My Friend Hardman by Ben Jones · · · · · · · · · · · · · · · 1
Chapter: 2 Ralph by Cynthia Williams · 10
Chapter: 3 Region of Innocence · 18
Chapter: 4 Letter to Kazuko c/o Bar Desire · · · · · · · · · · · · · · · 33
Chapter: 5 Excerpts from the Journal of a Sad,
             Fat Wordman · 35
Chapter: 6 Return of the Sad, Fat Organization Man · · · · · · · · 47
Chapter: 7 The Son of the Sad, Fat Wordman Goes North · · 56
Chapter: 8 Wind Sprints · 67

INTRODUCTION
BY LEE GOLDBERG

Six years ago, I fell in love with the twelve, out-of-print, *Hardman* crime novels by the late Ralph Dennis... an obsession that led me to acquire the copyright to his work, published and unpublished, and to co-found a publishing company to get his novels back into print.

His *Hardman* series, with numbered titles like *Hardman #1: Atlanta Deathwatch*, were all released in paperback in the mid-1970s by Popular Library, which packaged them as cheap, sleazy, men's action adventure novels. Most of the books in the genre were disposable hack work, slim volumes full of violence and sex with titles like *The Butcher* and *The Penetrator,* that were doomed to a short shelf life and oblivion.

But Ralph's *Hardman* novels were something different, terrific crime novels with nuanced characters, strong plots, a remarkable sense of place, and something meaningful to say about race relations in the deep south.

Even so, the novels slipped into obscurity and Ralph never achieved the recognition or success that he deserved, despite publishing three standalone novels outside of the series.

At the time of his death in 1988, Ralph was a destitute alcoholic, sleeping on a cot in the backroom of George's Deli in Atlanta and working as a clerk at a used bookstore.

However, Ralph wasn't entirely forgotten. His *Hardman* series remained beloved by crime writers, like novelist Joe R. Lansdale

(*Hap & Leonard*) and screenwriter Shane Black (*Lethal Weapon*), who credited Ralph for inspiring their work and who passionately recommended the yellowed, hard-to-find paperbacks to their friends.

In fact, that's how I discovered Ralph, because a friend made me read a Hardman novel. And I got hooked…bad.

When I set out to republish the *Hardman* novels, I recruited successful authors who were influenced by the series, as well as people who knew Ralph, to write essays for the new, reprint editions. Two of those essays in particular – one by his close friend Ben Jones, the actor and former U.S. Congressman from Georgia, and another by author Cynthia Williams, a former student of Ralph's who declined his marriage proposal — gave me revealing insight into the author I'd been investing so much of my time, effort, money and passion into editing and publishing.

I went on to substantially edit and republish his three stand-alone novels (*The War Heist* (aka *MacTaggart's War*), *The Broken Fixer* (aka *Atlanta*) and *A Talent for Killing* (aka *Dead Man's Game* combined with the previously unpublished sequel) and published his unsold manuscripts *The Spy in a Box* and *Dust in the Heart*. I'm pleased and proud to say that all of the books, the *Hardman* series and the standalones, received enthusiastic media reviews in the United States and abroad…the kind of literary respect and acclaim that he craved, and was sadly denied, in his lifetime.

At that point, I'd read virtually every novel, sold and unsold, that Ralph had written (except for two lost, unpublished manuscripts from the early 1960s). I'd noticed many recurring themes and plot situations in his books, particularly when it came to his portrayals of women, sex, and romantic relationships in general. After I read the essays by Ben and Cynthia, and traded lengthy emails with them, I was pretty sure I knew how Ralph's fiction mirrored the experiences and disappointments in his own life.

But I still wanted to learn more.

I knew from Ben and Cynthia, and from articles that I'd read, that Ralph was a student, and later an instructor, at the University of North Carolina at Chapel Hill during the 1960s. So, in the summer of 2019, I went to Chapel Hill on a research trip to read through Ralph's papers at the UNC library, to meet some of his old drinking buddies, and to see the places mentioned in his books.

I spent my days in the library's archives. I read the old issues of several Chapel Hill literary magazines that he'd contributed to first as a writer, and later as an editor, in the 1950s through the late 1960s. I read carbon copies of acceptance and rejection letters he sent to writers seeking publication in one of the magazines that he was editing. And I read the handwritten and typed letters that Ralph wrote in the 1970s, to his colleagues at UNC after he left Chapel Hill and moved to Atlanta, that chronicled some his early and later life as a novelist in the 1970s.

In the evenings, I spent time with some of Ralph's old friends, who shared with me what they knew about him and their insights into his life. I learned that Ralph, while still a student at UNC in the early 1960s, married a Chapel Hill woman who had a daughter from a previous relationship. Ralph graduated from UNC and moved his family to New Haven so he could pursue a Masters Degree in playwriting at Yale. Not long after arriving at Yale, his wife left him for another man. Ralph returned alone to Chapel Hill, where he ultimately received his Masters and stayed as a lecturer in the TV & film department.

I unearthed his marriage license and reached out to his ex-wife and step-daughter, both of whom kindly and honestly shared their memories of him with me.

I came away with a much deeper, richer, and nuanced understanding of Ralph Dennis as a man... and the many ways that his life influenced his writing.

Which brings me to this small collection of short stories which are, with one exception, laid out in the order in which they were originally published in various Chapel Hill literary magazines.

I selected the five stories and one poem in this book because of what they reveal about the man he was and the writer he would become.

The first story and the poem – *Region of Innocence* and *Letter to Kazuko c/o Bar Desire* – were among his earliest published works and were clearly inspired by actual experiences in his life as a soldier stationed in Japan in the 1950s.

His three *Sad Fat Wordman* stories, published between 1961 and 1967, are fascinating reflections of his own life and cover the period when he was a student and, five years later, an instructor at UNC. The *Sad Fat Wordman* stories are still fondly remembered by his friends for their humor and emotional impact more than fifty years after they were published.

Wind Sprints, the final story in this collection, which was published a few months before the third *Sad Fat Wordman* story, offers another revealing, emotional take on his life, his self-image, his failed marriage, and the child he left behind.

As an introduction to the stories, I've included the essays that Ben Jones and Cynthia Williams wrote for the *Hardman* novels to give you some of the same understanding and knowledge I had about Ralph when I first came upon, and read, the stories in this collection.

I hope you will find the stories as moving and provocative as I did...and that they will encourage you to seek out Ralph's incredible crime novels.

MY FRIEND HARDMAN

BY BEN JONES

If, on a late summer afternoon in 1973, you had walked into George's Deli on Highland Avenue in Atlanta, you would likely have seen a portly man in his 40's. He would have been on a barstool talking to his friend Sam Najar, the bartender. The customer is balding. It is all gone on top. He has sideburns that are beginning to show grey. His round, moustachioed face is pocked, and his Falstaffian beer gut cannot help but be noticed.

He is wearing a casual white short-sleeved shirt, khaki slacks, and brown loafers. If he knows you and likes you, he will ask you to join him at a booth. If your interests run to literature, writing, pop culture, film history, good wines and liquors, Japanese and Italian food, Southern ribaldry, or the traditionally American sports like baseball, football and basketball, you will soon realize that he knows more about all of these things than you do. And then you will start listening and learning. Because this guy, Ralph Dennis, is a great teacher.

From 1961 until his passing in 1988, Ralph was my friend, my mentor and my sidekick. In a few drunken instances, it fell to me to be his bodyguard. In those 27 years we had only one falling out, over a red-headed woman as it happened, and it was entirely my fault.

We had some things in common. I had grown up in a railroad section house without electricity or indoor plumbing by a railyard on the docks of Portsmouth, Virginia. Our shack was literally on the wrong side of the tracks in segregated Sugar Hill, then a bustling African American community. We were the only "white" folks in Sugar Hill. I know of that now as one of the great blessings of my life.

After a feckless high school career, I worked a series of odd jobs and saved up enough dough to enter East Carolina College in Greenville, North Carolina. While there, I saw a pamphlet about the Radio, Television, and Motion Pictures Department (RTVMP) at the University of North Carolina in Chapel Hill. I sent a handwritten letter to the UNC Admissions Department, and on the basis of that letter I was accepted. The Dean told me that they thought I had some writing talent.

One of the first courses I took was the survey course for RTVMP, a very large class in a vast auditorium. The graduate assistant who taught the writing section of that course was Ralph Dennis. He was very good at what he was doing, a fine and entertaining lecturer, and, though a bit droll and sardonic, he was never, ever boring. I liked his style, and related to his humor.

Most of the Chapel Hill drinking spots were clustered then on East Franklin St., directly across from the North entrance of the campus. But I had noticed a tavern some blocks west of there that piqued my interest, a place called Clarence's. It appeared to be more of a good old fashioned working man's beer joint.

The first time I walked in there, the only guy in there besides Clarence himself was Ralph. He seemed to be totally at home, as if he had lived there for some years.

I introduced myself. He was then 30 years old and I was 20. In that conversation and in thousands of others over the years, I learned a lot about Ralph, and a little bit about myself.

It was at Clarence's that we first bonded over a mutual appreciation of country music, sports, and film. We poured our beer change into the jukebox and as the regulars started coming in, I matched every Budweiser he drank with a Pabst Blue Ribbon, which was a nickel cheaper. He knew that I didn't have much dough, so he would spring for just about every other round. I realized early on that this was a *sympatico* relationship. We were both devoted to that old, but elusive, romantic notion of the artist's drinking life.

Like me, Ralph had come from a bone deep hardscrabble Southern raising. He didn't like to talk about it, but the story emerged over our shared years of lubricated conversation. Ralph was born in 1931, as the Great Depression was sinking ever harder into the American heartland. There were scars from those times that he clearly bore, but they were sealed and protected by a cranky, crusty, and often cynical attitude.

What had gotten him away from a future in the cotton mills was a High School teacher in his hometown of Sumter, South Carolina who recognized and encouraged his gifts of intelligence and writing talent. He spoke of her often as something of a savior.

After high school, Ralph joined the United States Navy, and headed to the Korean War. The highlight for him was a beautiful Geisha girl in Japan he lived with for a year or so. The lowlight was when an angry officer ordered him to drive a jeep across an airfield to his headquarters. Ralph jumped in and drove the jeep into a series of potholes and through a fence into a ditch. The irate officer didn't know that Ralph had never learned to drive. That fact made the officer even more furious.

"Then why in the hell did you do it?!" he yelled.

"Just following orders, sir," Ralph replied. "Just following orders."

And that was the first and last time that Ralph Dennis ever took the wheel of a vehicle.

He came home from Korea and Japan and used the G.I. bill and some scholarship money to pursue his writing ambitions. At Chapel Hill, he got an A.B. and a Masters, which he was working on when we met in the early 60's. There were some wild ass parties around there in those days, when sex, drugs, and rock and roll ruled the roost. Ralph got lucky with women now and then, didn't do any drugs other than alcohol and Pall Malls, and liked his music more nuanced and melodic than most. He was, after all, a bit older. And though it wasn't easy to pick up on, he was also a whole lot cooler than the folks who thought they were cool.

Ralph headed off to the Yale School of Drama for a doctorate somewhere around 1963. I got hitched to a gal from Texas and didn't pick up with Ralph until he got back in 1966. He had gotten another Masters, but he did not leave Yale under good circumstances. My attempts to find out what had transpired would end with a grunted comment about "an enormously stupid asshole." I understood. If nothing else, Ralph Dennis was a proud man, the kind of brilliant Southern country boy who knew what he was trying to do as a writer, and he knew how to do it. Apparently, he felt his Doctoral adviser was condescending and that the guy was trying to jack him around simply because he thought he could. Ralph told him to "put it where the moon don't shine."

There was also a woman up there, a very serious affair which had also ended badly. There was a lot more to it than that, but Ralph was reluctant to discuss it and I was just smart enough not to push it.

The University of North Carolina wanted him back, and he was glad to be back. His daily routine was simple. He would grind himself some good African or Brazilian Coffee, then walk to the campus from his modest apartment to teach at Swain Hall, home of the RTVMP Department. After classes, he would read and critique scripts, and when that was thoroughly finished, he would head to Jeff's Campus Confectionery to hang out with the other regulars who held court there, myself included. We drank a lot of beer in those days. I mean a hell of a lot of beer. We drank staggeringly prodigious , Homeric, Olympian Record amounts of beer.

Jeff's was a little newsstand with a bar in the back. There were no stools, but every day a truly diverse group of beer boozers would stand around for hours, rolling dice to see who was going to buy the next round. There were times when I'd knock off from my job waiting tables at Harry's Deli up the street and head for Jeff's. If I was lucky with the dice, I could drink for hours. There was an ancient bank safe in there, and it became my barstool. There was a bench in the back with a black and white 9 inch television set with extendable "rabbit ears" that someone had to hold and move around when the Tar Heel Basketball team was on.

If Ralph didn't show for a few hours, it was likely because he was working on a short story or some other writing project. He published some in small magazines, and he was at ground zero with the novelist Russell Banks' literary magazine, *Lillabulero*. I wrote a bit, and published a bit, but once I discovered I could make a little dough as an actor, I was hooked on the theatre.

I was in between marriages when I ended up in Atlanta in the fall of 1969. I got a union gig as an actor the day after I got off the bus. My Georgia girlfriend Mary Alice and I got hitched down in Briarpatch, Georgia, and we quickly found that there were a number of former Chapel Hillians in "Hotlanta", celebrating the New South and having a grand old time doing it.

By 1970, Ralph was "getting tired of students" and needed a change. It didn't take much to convince him that Atlanta had fully recovered from General Sherman and was a happening place. We drove up and got him and his belongings and helped him find a bachelor's pad. He got a regular job when his savings started to dwindle a bit, all the while writing every day. He wrote to his friend and agent Elizabeth McKee, pitching the idea for *Hardman*. Ms. McKee secured a contract with Popular Library.

Now, I wasn't there when it happened, but he was so overjoyed with the news that he ran the two and a half miles to our house so that he could tell somebody. Ralph Dennis had given up athletics in High School and was as out of shape as one would expect of a man who had downed 50 beers a week for 25 years, while chain-smoking Pall Malls.

But he made it. I wasn't at home, but Mary Alice was.

"I sold a book!!" he said.

Mary Alice said he was so happy that for years afterwards she found the moment thrilling. And I still can't help but smile when I think of that day.

Jim Hardman and Hump Evans were born that day. The books were excellent. They were the work of a thorough professional, working within a genre he greatly respected. Of course, Ralph had read all of Chandler and Hammett. But he seemed to have also read all of everyone else who ever put ink on paper: Tolstoy, Dostoyevsky, all of the Russians, all of the Classics and all of the Americans, Twain and Faulkner and especially Hemingway, whose style of carving out anything unnecessary was not lost on Ralph.

Ralph would write a first draft in two or three days. "Get the whole thing down as soon as you can," he told me. "The work is in the re-writing."

He loved to polish a sentence until there wasn't a trace of "fat" in it. He did the *Hardman* books with the work ethic of a coal miner, staying at it until there was nothing left to add or subtract.

Those streets and alleys of 1970's Atlanta have greatly disappeared now, paved under and over as a behemoth of a sprawling megalopolis has been birthed from the Georgia red clay; 14 lane super-highways circling through a maze of high-rise glitz and chrome. But if you know where to look…there was the Clermont Lounge…there was Plaza Drugs…there was the Stein Club…there was the "strip at Tight Squeeze".

Ralph and I were both alcoholics, but of a different sort. When I went on a binge, I couldn't stop until the game was over. As the old alkies say, "One drink is too many, a thousand isn't enough." But at a certain time in the evening, Ralph would say, "I need a lift home, I'm really 'schnokered'," and that would be that. I'd drop him off and go back out, looking for more trouble.

I was heading for a bad bottom in 1976. The Georgia lady had enough of my insanity and left. But the drinking got worse.

I got married again, and that hardly lasted longer than the first hangover. No one wanted to see me coming down the street.

Ralph and I argued over that red-headed woman and it caused a break in our long friendship. It was entirely my fault.

He got a book deal for *MacTaggart's War* (Editor's Note: Republished by Brash Books in 2019 as *The War Heist*) and went to England on the advance to do some research. I was making good money doing movie roles and spending it with no regard for anything except to be, as Dylan Thomas said, "the drunkest man in the World!"

I got sober in September of 1977. It was the start of another life for me. Soon afterwards Ralph tired of the Atlanta scene and went back up to Chapel Hill to write and teach. A year later, I was cast in the mega-hit TV series, *The Dukes of Hazzard*. My life changed so dramatically, that it seemed an entirely different life. It was and still is.

I didn't see Ralph for a couple of years, but we kept up through mutual friends. I sent him a letter of amends and he appreciated it. He was proud of how I had changed my ways and found some success.

After five years of sobriety and jumping cars in Hazzard County, I went up to Chapel Hill in 1982 when The Tar Heels were playing for the National Basketball Championship against Georgetown. The game was in New Orleans, but I knew the real action would be in Chapel Hill, especially if the Heels won. I went to where I knew Ralph would be, at Jeff's Campus Confectionery. He greeted me like the long-lost brother I was. He was drinking Michelob, I was drinking Diet Coke.

The Tar Heels won on a last second shot by Michael Jordan, a skinny 19-year-old freshman. The Victory celebration on Franklin Street was beyond wild, as it should have been.

Ralph returned to Atlanta the next year and to his stool at George's Deli. He got a job at the Oxford bookstore and kept writing. When I was in town, I'd pick up Ralph and we'd hit the

Atlanta Braves or Hawks games, me drinking green tea, and him downing Budweisers.

When *The Dukes of Hazzard* ended in 1985, I asked Ralph to come up with an idea for an Atlanta detective series. I said that the *Hardman* series would make a terrific television show. He agreed, but he felt I wasn't right to play Jim Hardman. And then he said something that seemed to come from a deeper place.

"Hardman is 'in'." he told me. "But you are 'out'."

I think he was saying that I had escaped from my addictions and my despair, but that Hardman (and Ralph) had not and likely never would.

Instead, he did a half-dozen, two-page outlines of possible stories, and a full treatment for a pilot episode, for a different detective series called *Gunnarson*. Steve Gunnarson was a former jock and Special Forces guy who had inherited the family bookstore, which specialized in rare books and maps. The other side of "Gunnarson, the Hardass" was "Gunnarson, the thoughtful Renaissance Man." Gunnarson "did favors" for friends with problems, a sort of dangerous hobby. I thought the time was right for an Atlanta show. (I played on a softball team there with Isaac Hayes, and we wrote a part for him.)

I pitched *Gunnarson* to CBS in that same endless line with everyone else in Hollywood who could "get a meeting". Nothing happened. It rarely does out there. I think they were just being courteous.

In 1986, I was approached by the State Democratic Party to see if I was interested in running for Congress. "I've got more bones in my closet than the Smithsonian Institute," I told them. But the Party was desperate. And a lot of folks, including Ralph, told me that I didn't really have anything to lose and that I should jump in just for the hell of it. Ralph wrote my first political speech. He had never written one, and I had never given one. I almost won the race, and ran again in 1988.

George's Deli on Highland Ave. was smack in the middle of that District and I would stop in to see Ralph whenever I had a few minutes. He was having some health problems and job problems and was crankier than ever. While Ralph was looking for a new apartment, George was letting him sleep on a cot in the back of the place. During one night, he had a seizure of some sort and was found in a coma the next morning. He was rushed to Crawford Long Hospital near death, but recovered enough to have several female visitors a couple of days later. Then it went the other way. The day before he died I spent time at his bedside with his kid sister Irma, who flew in from Michigan. He died on July 4th, 1988, as fireworks exploded everywhere above Atlanta.

When I won that '88 race, I knew that he was as proud as hell of me, as if I was his kid brother. And in a way I surely was.

One day, a few months before he passed, he went into an eloquent chat about the English writer and critic Cyril Connolly. He quoted Connolly as saying, "Inside every fat man there is a thin man wildly signaling to get out." And then, "Whom the Gods wish to destroy, they first call promising."

In one of our last talks, Ralph, deep in his cups, told me of how, at the height of the Great Depression, his mother had taken him and his kid brother and sister and put them out at a state orphanage. He remembered the gates closing. He was about seven years old.

"Sometimes I still get the feeling of watching that car pull away from us," he said. He had never mentioned that before.

Ben Jones is an actor, singer, writer, and recovering politician who lives on a farm in the Blue Ridge Mountains of Virginia. His memoir Redneck Boy in the Promised Land *was published by Random House. He served in the U.S. House of Representatives as a Congressman from Georgia. He has appeared in countless productions and films, but is surely best known as the affable mechanic "Cooter" on the hit television series* The Dukes of Hazzard.

RALPH

BY CYNTHIA WILLIAMS

I knew Ralph Dennis first as a teacher, and later as a friend and mentor. Eventually, he asked me to marry him, but I refused, and our friendship ended.

Obviously, I will remember Ralph differently from the men who knew him, because he was, in some ways, a different person with me.

I met Ralph Dennis in 1966. I was in my junior year at UNC Chapel Hill, majoring in Radio, Television and Motion Picture Production (RTVMP), and as my rather vague intent was to become a screenwriter for motion pictures, I took Mr. Dennis's screenplay writing classes. He was a good teacher, because I still remember the mechanics of writing a film script, yet all I remember of the classes is Ralph sitting on the edge of his desk, coffee cup in one hand and a cigarette in the other, his face expressionless, occasionally flicking cigarette ash at an ashtray. In retrospect, I suspect he may have been bored. Possibly hung over. I liked him. He was cool. I saw him as a Hemingway-esque kind of writer. Undoubtedly, he did, too.

After I graduated in 1968, some circumstance I don't recall brought me back to Chapel Hill while Ralph was still teaching. I remember only that we met in his hangout, a small bar on the downslope of west Franklin Street. Ralph sat across the booth from me and my young husband, clearly uncomfortable.

I intuited that I should not have brought Dewey with me. I came away from the meeting with an inexplicable sense of dissatisfaction, the feeling that I had embarrassed the man—or worse, bored him.

Four or five years later, in 1974, I was divorced, living in east central Tennessee, and working on my first novel. By this time, Ralph had left UNC and was living some 200 miles away from me in Atlanta, trying to make it as a self- supporting writer. I have no idea how I knew where he was, unless we had kept up some kind of occasional correspondence. So many links are missing from my recollections of this time that I can scarcely connect the dots between one event and the next. Not that it matters. All I know is that over the next two years, I drove down to Atlanta a few times to spend a weekend carousing with Ralph and friends of his (including that insanely funny Ben Jones) at George's Deli.

I recall his apartment as being one large room above a garage. As you walked in, his writing desk was to your right. To your left was a small bathroom. Beyond that, to the left, a book case and against the far wall a single- size bed. There must have been some kind of cooking facility and a table because on the one occasion I visited him there, he made shrimp scampi for me—shrimp sautéed in butter with scallions—served with a cold white wine.

I must have brought my unfinished manuscript with me that day, because I remember sitting on the edge of his bed while he sat at his desk reading it. I dared not even look at him while he read.

Finally, he stirred. I put my face in my hands as he got up with the manuscript in his hand and walked across the room to me. He stood over me with his gentle smile. "Lady," he said, "this is a hardback."

We walked in the park across the street one brisk, bright, golden autumn day. Ralph was rather stiffly polite, so I think it was probably during my first visit to him there. In my company, he was always a gentleman. Kind. Gentle. Smiling. Perhaps in deference to my youth and obvious naiveté. I was intelligent and well- educated, but when it came to knowing men, I was dumb as a post.

I was beautiful, you see, with a voluptuous body of which I was oblivious. I was entirely cerebral, impassioned with the life of the intellect. In my eyes, Ralph was still my teacher. He was sending me the books he said were required reading if I seriously wanted to learn how to write. The first book he sent me was Dostoyevsky's *The Idiot*. Told me to read it every year, as he did. He introduced me to Turgenev with *A Sportsman's Sketches*. All of the titles on his reading list were classics, heavy, rich literature. I wallowed in them with such pleasure, with an insatiable appetite for learning.

And I was excited by his interest in me as a writer.

The seduction he practiced upon me was patient. Patiently, over a cheesy French onion soup with a bottle of strong, raw Chianti, he listened, smiling, to my passionate opinions about God-knows-what-all. When he spoke, always quietly and deliberately, I was an eager listener. He must have been encouraged by the warm light in my eyes, unsuspecting that it was the glow of admiration, perhaps affection, but not desire.

Every morning while our friendship lasted, he wrote a letter to me. Called it his ten- finger exercise—a warm- up for the day's writing. I have none of the letters he wrote to me, and of them, I recall only one; he described a recent date involving "one of those sweaty, candlelight suppers" that Southern women insisted upon. Ralph was a disciplined writer and he had to be, because his income from the *Hardman* books depended on the quantity of his output. He was clearly embarrassed to be writing for money, restless and angry at the necessity of it, hoping to make enough from the *Hardman* books to support himself while he wrote some serious hardbacks. He described his life as being a routine of writing by day and drinking beer at George's by night.

Ralph sent me copies of all the *Hardman* books with affectionate inscriptions, but like the Valentine's Day gift of *The Romantic Egoists*, a wonderfully illustrated, coffee table biography of Scott and Zelda Fitzgerald, I let them go with the rest of my library, which I sold in 2011.

The man was a hopeless romantic. He called me one day while I was visiting my brother and his wife in Asheville. Said, "Listen to this," put the phone receiver down by his stereo and left it there all the way through Carmina Burana. Like the literature he shared with me, it was glorious. We were both mind- swerving drunk on it. I was enormously flattered by his attention, by the obvious fact that he had fallen in love with me. I was 28 and writers were my heroes and he was a writer. Again, I lived in my head, and again, for a young woman my age, and a divorcée, no less, I was unbelievably stupid about men. I had no sexual interest in Ralph Dennis, so I ignored his in me. For a long time, he had the good sense, apparently, not to attempt to pressure me into a sexual relationship. As I say, the seduction he practiced upon me was subtle and patient.

Unless his reticence with me was reluctance. He was a balding man with a beer belly in love with a beautiful young thing nearly half his age. He may simply have dreaded my response to any overt demonstration of sexual desire. So, he bided his time.

What he had going for him, and he knew it, was my admiration for his intellect, his self-confidence and skill as a writer.

His Christmas gift to me in 1975 was a solid gold pocket watch with an inscription dated 1906. The watch was slender, as if designed to rest in the palm of a lady's hand. It was exquisite and adored it. But I remember that, as I sat alone by my Christmas tree one night, turning the golden wafer of a timepiece this way and that to reflect the colored lights on the tree, I felt inexpressibly sad. The gift was expensive and fairly radiated Ralph's love for me, and I knew that I did not love him the way he wanted me to and that I should not accept the gift. It was his very declaration of love. I gazed at it ticking softly in the palm of my hand, shimmering.

In hindsight, I realize that, with the gift of the watch, our relationship shifted. Ralph became supplicant. I think it was a couple of months later that Ralph took me to an expensive restaurant in downtown Atlanta and ordered a large plate of oysters oreganata for each of us. I was embarrassed to have to admit that I could not eat oysters (they looked like phlegm on the half shell to me). Ever the compliant gentleman, he ordered me something else and when we left the restaurant, handed the carry-out box of oysters to a homeless man outside the restaurant.

Why in God's name I felt I had to go shopping that afternoon for a lipstick liner I will never know, but we stepped into a department store and while I was at the cosmetic counter, he disappeared. Back outside on the sidewalk in front of the store, he pulled a jewel box from his pocket and opened it. Inside was the largest, most luscious opal (my birthstone) and diamond ring that has ever sparkled before my eyes. He offered it to me as an engagement ring.

I couldn't take it. Although in my selfish desire for his friendship I had ignored all the signs of his having fallen in love with me, I was neither a cruel nor a dishonest young woman.

I was embarrassed, so I hedged at first, saying the ring was much too expensive. He ignored that, urging me to put it on. I must have convinced him that I was not ready to marry again, because he finally went back in the store and returned it. I felt he was trying to force me, as if the extravagance and sheer richness of the gift would prove irresistible, but if he thought so, he did not know me. And although the gesture had discomforted, even irritated me, I have never forgotten the disappointment in his eyes when he closed the box and turned with it back into the store.

He was a sad man. Even in my memories of the fun times, of boozy laughter in smoke-filled bars, I remember him as being quiet, reserved, yet smiling, his eyes amused, and if shaken occasionally with chuckles, I don't remember him participating in our uproarious shouting and laughter. In hindsight, I realize that he was a lonely, middle-aged man watching kids having fun.

Behind the amusement, the sad man waited, watching, defeated. He had been defeated all his life by women who did not want him.

When I was in his apartment, I saw a framed photo of a little boy on a pony. Grinning, I asked if it were a picture of him. He nodded. I think he told me then that he had been orphaned very young. I learned only recently, in reading Ben Jones's, *My Friend Hardman*, that Ralph Dennis had siblings and that their mother had left them in an orphanage when he was six or seven years old. That he remembered watching, through the bars of a closing gate, his mother drive away.

I believe that a child abandoned by his mother will carry within himself always the expectation of rejection, that he will lack the sense of self- worth that is essential to achievement— be his goal winning the love of a woman or winning a Pulitzer. I believe that Ralph Dennis, for all his intellect and education and his skill and confidence as a writer, expected defeat. His very posture was that of a defeated man.

I realize now that as a twenty- something, I intuited his sadness, his hopelessness; I knew that his need for me was emotional; I sensed that he wanted to marry me because he needed to own me. I had the vague idea that, if I married him, I would effectively become the prisoner of a jealous and controlling man.

I lost respect for him. I hotly resisted his attempts to hobble me. To bind me. He'd call me on the phone, arguing his case. He wrote me long letters. Said that if I didn't want to marry him, I could just live with him.

His need was an irritant. Like a fly touching my cheek, my shoulder, the back of my hand. Finally one day, I sat down at my electric typewriter and furiously typed a letter that stated my feelings in no uncertain terms. I remember the white hot fury with which I typed that day, the soot-black marks of the ink ribbon upon the white typing paper, and I remember a bit of the phone call I received a few days later. He said that my letter had been "hammering letter," that it was "castrating."

 We had a heated exchange. I was shocked and contemptuous of his feeling of having been castrated by my refusal to marry him. Asserted (truthfully) that I had no idea what he was talking about, that if he thought a woman's refusal to marry him was castrating, then he had a real problem, and so on and on, back and forth, until he said goodbye and I knew that he would never speak to me again.

 And but for one short and final sentence, he never did. A year or so later, I was in Atlanta again visiting the woman who had been one of the gang in the drunken glory days at George's. I took a notion to go to George's, hoping I'd catch Ralph there and that we could, I don't know, hug like old friends again. Something like that. Who knows what the hell I wanted.

 Just to see him, say hey, be friends again. I could have had no idea how deeply my rejection had cut him.

 Sure enough, he was at the bar talking with another man when we came in. We took our seats at a booth. He gave no sign that he had seen us. I was fairly bouncing with excitement, so happy to see him again.

 Finally, he walked over to the table. I looked up with an eager grin, and he said, "I said goodbye to you a year ago, lady."

 The coldness of his eyes stunned me, literally stopped my breath. I don't know whether he turned and went back to the bar or walked out. I don't remember anything after that.

 I grew up eventually. Now I understand. Now I know. And I can tell you this much: Ralph Dennis was not Hardman. Hardman was the man he wished to be.

Cynthia Williams is a professional writer whose work includes creative non-fiction, fiction, narrative history, and copy writing for television. She is the author of Hidden History of Fort Myers *and the children's book* Me and the Sky. *Cynthia has also recently completed a screenplay for an animated film titled* Happy.

"When Ralph Dennis came to the University in 1955, he had a purpose of sorts. Like most veterans coming here on the Korean G.I. Bill, he was a little short of cash, long on determination, and impatient at what appeared to be the leisurely pace of faculty and students....

From the moment he walked into his first class, professors and students knew there wasn't much he wasn't going to challenge. By the time he took his degree in English with honors in writing, he had a small but devoted following of younger students all his own.

And he wrote."
— from *The Chapel Hill Weekly,* August 1, 1963, in an article entitled *Dennis Plans Year of Study at Yale.*

"Out of the Navy, he enrolled at the University of North Carolina. Soon, he entered a short-fiction contest. His story was about a group of sailors on leave in a red-light district. The prize had been put up by an elderly woman in memory of her daughter. Ralph won. When the donor read the winning story, she withdrew the prize. Ralph did get his $100, however. 'I threw a great $100 beer party,' he recalled."
— from *The Atlanta Constitution,* June 30, 1974, in an article entitled *Mind if I Kill You Off in Chapter Three? Atlanta Writer Spins Tales of Violence Among the Peachtrees.*

REGION OF INNOCENCE

This story was published in the Carolina Quarterly *in 1955 and was the first place winner of their fifth annual fiction award. The Quarterly's editor had this to say at the time: "In the opinion of the judges,* Region of Innocence *is a powerful story well told, although marred by a certain heavy-handedness of style."*

There is a paved road that goes erratically through the Naval Air Station and into the low farm land where the stooped women plant the tender rice shoots. It is a good road; for the country it is a magnificent road. In that mile in the spartan farmyards, rice is husked in a flat drum turned manually. The kernels are laid out to dry on woven straw mats. In the fields a honey bucket boy dips human excreta into the flooded squares of new rice plants. The men may stop to watch a vehicle pass; the women work steadily on, bending into the deep mud.

At the end of this mile, the road has almost terminated; to the left the highway abruptly joins a pitted clay path that leads to Otsuka Hommachi; to the right another four hundred yards before the jarring ruts and ridges and the first squat buildings of Sagami Otsuka.

There are roughly seventy bars, two grocery stores, and a combination bus-train station in this town. There is a fluent population of nearly four hundred young girls, a *mama-san* and a *papa-san* for each bar, and for some of the better bars, a male bartender.

The bars lean and crowd and elbow toward the bus station, where at four and five and six o'clock the early sailors begin their nightly prowling with an urgency, a pent-up sounding that shells and husks the buildings and the people.

In the year 1954 in early May came two sailors burnt very brown from another sun. They were eager to begin the months of feasting orgy that were to make them separate, nearly hostile, and were to begin the cocoon age, a delicate age.

I am the taller of the two, twenty-three years of age, a Southerner. I will be my own conscience; this is not my story, except the fringe area, the crust. My friend is younger, nineteen. His home is somewhere in the region of innocence. His hair is crisp, blond, dark at the temple edges. He is a length of spring steel.

There is a cool wind up the mud street; the dips and ruts lease a fetid odor. The afternoon rain pools in the untouched outer lengths. Two children (I have not previously counted children) leap about and shout in an open field. They are awkward in the cheap wooden *geta*.

Our blood has thinned in the constant heat of the Marianas. The wind has a chill and the open frankness of a knife blade. We have two quick whiskies in the nearest bar while two *josons* eye us invitingly. We give the positive no as we move out into the evening traffic of already drunk sailors. We shiver in the thin whites.

"My God, and this is supposed to be spring." He blew into his cupped hands.

"This might be a frozen scene," I answer, "where two sailors are found as ice blocks in skivvy town."

"Maybe one of these places has some kind of heat." He lit a cigarette and cupped his hands over the glow. I nodded a negative to a *joson* leaning interested in a doorway. She will collar the next sailor.

This is not of our making; circumstances conspire. The next bar is heated ... a small gas jet dangerously between two cushioned benches. A Japanese boy mixed our drinks while Fred and I leaned over the heater. We laughed out of relief and partly out of amusement.

"Dammit. I knew there was one in town." This from Fred before the rear door opened and two *josons* entered. Then a silence. The phonograph in the corner of the room had ended a scratchy Glenn Miller. The buxom girl placed the drinks before us and collected the yen, bending from the hips for the sake of cleavage (being indiscriminate, a view for each of us).

The slender girl gave us only the barest of looks as she passed to the phonograph. Another Glenn Miller. A rustle of her skirt and she had crowded my bench. The buxom girl took the obvious seat.

She had in fact taken three-quarters of it. Fred, thin-flanked, braced himself against the wall.

"Cornered, aren't we?" A frightened, jumpy smile at his lips. "Unless we want to make an exit out of the side of the house."

I looked at the slender girl, turning in my seat. Her smile was the grandmother of smiles, a disease at twenty-two and twenty-three.

"Well, dammit, make the most of it. This is the only heater in town."

I took her left breast in the shovel of one hand, the nipple hard against my thumb. Mute, very mute, a dumbness in her eyes.

"What's your name, *joson*"

"Kazuko. Sometime they say Judy." Her smile was then suddenly a wide grin. I had shown interest, a definite intent. She bound my knee in a gnome's hand. She offered, leaning toward me, the clean rice breath.

Across the table, Fred had become as stiff as two-fifth's full; his eyes had a wounded quality.

"How long you stay Sagami, Kazuko?"

"Maybe one year."

"One year *domi*, no good."

Now there were two wounded people at the table. I decided to joke. I lit a cigarette.

"Navy *domi* too. I stay Navy maybe three years." No response. I drank my drink rapidly.

"You want drink?" She was still wounded; a thought for the *mama-san's* sake.

"*Hai*. Fred, you want another?"

"Yes. Vo and water."

"Two vo and water, *dozo*, Kazuko."

Fred moved the buxom *joson* and slid off the bench. "Red, let's try the head." He went in front of me through the rear door and into the narrow passageway.

He said, "I don't really want to go to the head. How do you ask price with these hogs?"

"Just say: How much you speak. And give her about three hundred less than she asks." I wanted to laugh; instead I went into the head and threw my cigarette butt into the urinal. When I came back, he had cornered his *joson* at the bar. She was on him like a chest plaster; all was well.

Kazuko was huddled at the phonograph, her back to me but one ear turned slightly. I stood at the wooden half-oval and drank half of the drink. Fred and the *joson* had arrived at a price. They braced their hips together and went through the back entrance.

"Kazuko." I spoke gently. "*Koko, dozo*."

She was against me suddenly, arms up and reaching. "You stay tonight, *ne*?"

"*Hai*. How much you speak?" I finished the drink and began turning the empty glass in a circular motion.

"Maybe 1800 yen."

"I give maybe 1400 yen."

"I speak 1500 yen."

I nodded and her tongue moved into my ear. In the passageway we turned right onto a small cement platform. She removed her shoes, then my own. We stepped up to a polished hardwood hall and went down it in complete darkness to her room. I waited while she fumbled with the light cord.

The room was nearly monastic. There was a bed and there was a low shelf at the foot of the bed whereon was perched a wedding doll. On the walls were two pictures torn from a movie magazine thumbtacked at an angle. One corner was curtained off to serve as a closet. There was a nightstand and a pan of water, a clock that was fifteen minutes fast. Bar clocks and cathouse clocks are always fast.

I watched her with a new pity as she folded her clothes in the small cube with barely room to turn about. Then the rough skin of her breasts and the thin flanks... and closer the perfumed oil scent bruising my nostrils...

After the heat, the whole pain, she slept. She curled toward me warmly, warmly. The clock had a loud ungodly tick. There was no sleep now.

Two rooms down I listened for the invisible membrane, the snap, the pop, the crackle.

Outside, two sailors howl and kick to pieces a latticed window.

⚜ ⚜ ⚜

I sweated in the bomb bay of No. 20, pulling a micro switch out of the bomb door warning system. Drops ran down my nose and collected in my mustache; other rivulets left my chin and pooled a ring around my feet.

I cursed loudly, vehemently. Fred dipped under the bomb doors dressed in whites and liberty neckerchief. He held the flashlight patiently while I disconnected the leads and collected the tools. We dodged an AF taxiing toward the tower. The strip lights went on and the beacon light began sweeping from above the tower.

I said, "Wait until I finish this up and I'll take in Sagami with you."

"Maybe." He flipped the flashlight back and forth in his hands, almost fiercely. As we passed through the readyroom, the night crew first class called from the far corner, "What does it look like?"

"Probably the switch. Know in a minute."

I flipped on the light in the electric shop and took down a meter. Fred squatted on an instrument can in the corner near the door. I zeroed the meter and connected the leads. The nipple of the switch made a brittle noise in the vacuum, the total silence.

"Red, I'm gonna shack with Chieko starting tonight. She seems a pretty good head."

"Why tell me?" I watched the instrument face.

"Wanted to know what you thought of it."

The first class opened the door. "How does it look?"

"Bad switch. Take a few minutes to get a new one in."

"Paynight. I secured the rest of the crew. We'll try it out after you get the new one in." The first class closed the door.

"You'll be at the Mood, won't you?" I ripped the waterproofing off the new switch.

"For a while," Fred answered.

"Wait for me. I'll bring a wedding present."

He banged his fist against the wall and roared, "It's not the same, is it?"

"Almost." I lit a cigarette and began collecting the tools. "You're about to make a fool out of yourself. You just learned what candy tastes like and you want to buy the candy shop. What happens if you buy a chocolate shop and later on want to try mint? You'll play hell, boy. These women act like the chaplain made the shack job. You butterfly on them and they'll cut your chimpo off and feed it to you."

"Sounds like a scare story. That's more the exception than the rule."

"I'd hate like hell to have an exceptional soprano voice." I pocketed the crescent, the boxend, the rachet, and the screwdriver. "Give me about an hour to get to the Mood."

Fred toed the instrument can back into position and rammed the light switch down. Violence near the surface. We went outside. Fred circled the hangar to catch the station bus to the gate. I started across the taxi strip toward No. 20. The sweeping beacon lighted for an instant the dormant shapes of aircraft, the cable tiedowns, the canvas shrouds.

On the landing strip, a squadron of jets practiced night carrier landings. In front of the tower, a plane loaded for Honolulu.

A shade over an hour later, the cab drew abreast of the Mood. I yelled at the driver but it was fifty feet forward and directly above a mud lake when he braked the taxi. I paid the hundred-fifty yen and stepped into the shallowest pool. I swung the sacked bottle against my thigh. There was the same overpowering stench, the outhouse or *benjo* and the residue of the casual halting of *papa-san* along the street.

A marine lurched out of the Mood missing the step up and barely righting himself. A bottle spun out of his fist and rolled over in the mud. Scooping it up, he drank the last thimbleful and hurled the bottle across the street into an alley. Seeing me, he muttered, "Good old Sagami mud."

"Just like chocolate candy," I answered.

Fred was morosely drinking a Nippon beer at the far end of the bar, one elbow on the record collection. One of the *josons* recognized me and hurried through the rear door. Kazuko must be catching short times, I thought.

Fred had not seen me. I said hello to George, the bartender, and slammed the bottle down by Fred's elbow.

I said, "Happy birthday." And then, "A Nippon for me too, George."

Fred said, "You took a helluva time getting here."

The Nippon came and I poured out the first glass.

Grinning I said, "I told the driver to stop when we passed the Mood but we were in front of the baths in Yamoto before he did."

The first glass carried off the silt collected during the day. I poured the second.

"It's warming up outside; this is a hell of a time to shack."

"It's the only time I've got."

Kazuko stepped down through the front door. Her face was damp and her small breasts rose in uneven stride. "Hello, *Red-san*," she said close to my ear. I got a clotted nostril of the perfumed oil.

"*Kombawa*, Kazuko." I was unmoved. Nothing about her touched me. I asked Fred, "Where's Chieko?"

"Tying up a few bundles. She found a place in Otsuka Hommachi."

"You see it yet?"

"No, but she says it's okay. Two rooms and a community *benjo*."

"Well, anyhow, you drink this damn whiskey I brought you."

He lifted it out of the sack and looked at the label. I. W. Harper.

"I appreciate the gift, but you still don't like it, do you?"

"I don't have any right not to like it. You should have picked an uglier one."

Kazuko poured the bottom of the bottle into my glass and stood at my shoulder. It was hot; her perfume lumped and rolled into my ears; it caked my hair.

"Maybe you stay tonight, *Red-san*?"

The impressive front of Chieko came in the front door a couple of seconds before she did.

"I have taxi. We go now," she said.

Fred gulped his drink and went out through the thick morass toward the cab. I followed and stood on the cement fronting to the bar. I shouted, "Lucky, *boy-san*," as the cab door slammed and the driver clashed gears before the Ford began the rough passage toward the four hundred yards of good highway and the clay path to Otsuka Hommachi.

Kazuko said, "Maybe you stay tonight."

"Maybe I stop later."

In this hour of beginnings I began a weaving progress toward Bar Clover where there were four girls oddly named Peanuts, Popcorn, Cracker jack, and Candy.

⚜ ⚜ ⚜

It was a good three weeks before I caught Fred again. We were in the same duty section but we were working different shifts. When he secured at 1630, I began the night's work. It was a sort of "Hi Red, Hi Fred" arrangement. I'd come out of the chow hall at 1715 just in time to see him heading out of the barracks with a bag of coffee or a present under one arm and his neckerchief hanging untied under the neckpiece of his jumper.

I'd say, "How's the love-life?"

And he'd say, "Fine. The greatest," with a grin that was three-quarters of his face ...

This day I had awakened at noon in the upper bedroom of the Colorado with my nose deep in the hair of someone named Kate. This was not material. But through the window directly behind me poured all the dirty rain in Honshu. From the depth of the poolings, it had evidently been raining for hours. An old mama-san or two stepped over the worse spots. There was a clatter of *geta*. A train debauched a stampede of children returning from school. The children were a legion of bright umbrellas passing.

There seemed to be no lessening in the thick, punitive fall. *Nyubai*, the rainy season. There would be no squadron planes in the air today. There would be a quick muster at five and a quicker bus back to Sagami.

"Kate," I said patting her backside, "maybe I come back tonight."

Back at the Station, after I had thrown my hat on my sack and picked up a letter from under my pillow, I went into the rec room. Fred was seated at the bench-table working crossword puzzles. Some joker had picked a Japanese station on the radio, a cultural concert consisting of man and *samisen*. A fine imitation of a cat with his tail tied to a harp.

I took a seat on the opposite side of the bench and opened the letter. "You going native, Fred?"

"In a small way," he replied.

"Really lap this noise up, eh?"

"Sure, man, wake up to it every morning."

I read the letter, skipping my eyes over it impatiently.

"That roundeye still love you, *boy-san*?"

Fred closed the book of puzzles.

"Sure. She said she was glad I wasn't having anything to do with those *josons* because she had heard they were filthy."

I refolded the letter and deposited it in my waistband. Someone had turned on the heat; the radiator hissed and chuckled. The drains on the streets were not channeling off the water fast enough. The falling rain was slanted heavily in the wind.

I said, "Anything to do at the squadron tonight?"

"Number 12 was supposed to come from Itasuki for a 120-hour check but it's too wet for flying."

"Well, Fred, what's with you? I thought all shackrats were making a run for home."

"I got the duty."

"So has the section leader, but I bet he's halfway to the Mile High by now."

"I don't believe in that, Red."

"I see. Just because they don't pick up liberty cards is no reason for Jack Armstrong, the All-American boy, to hit the beach."

I lit a cigar. "If it was me, maybe I could see staying aboard, but boy, you've got it paid for."

The first class stopped in the doorway with his muster sheet.

"You can muster me, Webb; I think Beet and the cripple are sacked out in the dorm."

"Nothing to do tonight, but there's a big night tomorrow."

He went away.

I braced my weight against the window frame and saw in the heavy downpour the Japanese office girls leaving the Ship Service building. For every hog there are ninety-nine nice girls in this goddamn country. We know the hogs by scent and touch and sound; the decent women to us are not tangible people. Umbrellas, short boots, they wear.

"You got something on tonight, Red?" Fred asked.

"Not exactly, though I did almost promise Kate I'd bless her again."

"How about coming over to my place and cracking a bottle of *sake*?"

"Fine," I said, "if you let me buy it."

He nodded and swung his legs over the bench. "As soon as I get a shower."

The Sagami Railway Company is a single track system with two-track loading at the station. At seven o'clock there is usually a profusion of office type workers on both sides of the tracks. We arrived a few minutes after seven and the platforms were empty. I consulted the timetable and the station keeper's clock.

"About twenty minutes," I said.

We caught a quart of Nippon in the San Francisco while an early combo of Japanese boys mangled the hell out of Gershwin.

I said, "This is much better than Rice-Paddy Pete and his three-string *samisen*."

The combo left Gershwin bleeding and picked up on Flying Home. The man on the baritone sax was rough, pure granite. Three or four sailors looked up from their *josons* and the undercover work and began to shout, "Go, man, go."

The bartender belatedly plugged in a motor that began to color the room with a spinning gelatin wheel, pinks, ambers, greens, and blues. The combo took on a note of frenzy, an orgiastic mood.

"I bet they think this is the real high class."

"For this part of the country, it probably is." He drank his beer moodily.

We were on the platform a minute before we heard the train from Yokohoma or saw the headlight pass the bend. Two office girls spoke *sayonara* across the tracks with a lilt and a softness. The rain had lessened a bit; umbrellas were folded.

The train from Ebina took the far track and swished its doors. Our train moved into place and we boarded it with rough force in the Japanese fashion.

There was not much to watch on the five-minute ride. The women we had seen before, the "business girls" who were returning from the hot baths in Yamoto, the office girls who were somehow intangible, yet interested, and the farm women coarse-skinned and stooped in the shoulders. The young men are sullen; the old men are like broken matches. By agreement, Fred and I watched the dark fields and the flat low hovels.

A passage of ten minutes up a mud lane and a steep climb, we walked through a stone arch and into a courtyard. Along the perimeter of the courtyard were the shapes of bushes and flower beds. In the far right corner was a rectangular building which was completely right angles. Two sliding paper doors. A clothes line.

"Two sailors shack there with two sisters," Fred said. "Just like a big happy family."

The main building was a farmhouse, two storeys high. It had never been painted; it had weathered to a dull brown finish. The far left corner of this building had a sliding door paned with glass. We entered in the darkness and removed our shoes on a small concrete block before stepping into the hall. Then a narrow wooden ladder to the second floor.

Fred said, "The light's out. Chieko's either in the pad or at one of these slopehead movies."

Then through another door and into a small cubicle. There was a table, an oil burner, and utensils racked on the wall.

"The kitchen," he said. "I'll see if Chieko has any clothes on." The scrape of another door, the jangle of a light cord missed and then caught and then a strong light. Silence for a minute.

Then Fred said, "Red, you go down the street to the Hideaway. I'll be there in five minutes."

I said, "What the hell for?" and started into the room. Then I heard Chieko cry out and then a deeper voice wake in surprise.

"Go ahead, Red. I'll be there in a few minutes."

I turned and opened the sliding door and closed it gently behind me. I heard Fred say, "You scoop-jawed whore," then "That's all right, you just drag your butt."

Then I was standing outside the front door with my shoes in one hand and the *sake* in the other.

Chieko screamed something in Japanese and the light went on in the *mama-san's* room on the lower deck.

I put on my shoes and went under the arch and down the steep hill nearly running. The night had suddenly a warm stench. I walked until there was no more sound from the farmhouse. There was only the drunken movement of an old *papa-san* who had missed a steep turn and had walked into a ditch.

There is a final summation to be made. The period of incubation, the cocoon age (a delicate age) must be recognized as ended. Out of the husk had come the wings and the inclination toward flight. In the following weeks, there was constant flight and constant disorder. He had brought his gear back from the house in Otsuka Hommachi and stowed it away in his locker with very little comment. He was unbelievably calm in the squadron area and in his infrequent visits to the barracks. But here the calm ended. Nearly every night he followed a trail that began at the bars nearest the bus station and ended in the bed he entered after eleven o'clock. I offered no comment, no censure. The road to hell is a private speedway.

In a small way he became famous in the town. As we plodded through the ruts and dips of the streets and paths, the *mama-sans* and the *josons* would spill out into the bar fronts and cross their wrists and move their hands in a butterfly gesture. They would shout, "Butterfly. Butterfly boy-san," in shrill voices, one quarter amusement, three-quarters contempt. Fred assumed at these moments the sickly sweet expression seen on the faces of movie stars before their public and said in a low side voice, "Hell, isn't it?"

This led to the weekend in Yokohoma where he had tattooed across the back of his right hand a dull yellow butterfly with jade webbing. The operation occurred during a drunk that began late one Friday night, was nurtured through the following morning in the room of an especially ugly *joson*, and continued through Saturday night in a number of bars and through several short times caught with several different girls with only a minimum of passion. There was a pause Saturday night in the tattoo shop. A withered old *papa-san* bent over his hand and sketched out the design. He bowed and smiled often. During the whirring of the needle, Fred cursed and argued and said his single Japanese word, "*Ichiban*," over and over. I standing, rather leaning, in the doorway (sick, very sick, disgusted) offered him dryly another Japanese word as the butterfly took shape.

Fred showed me proudly the finished product before it was to be bandaged by the old man. "Really something, ain't it?" he asked.

I turned away and started down the street without him, but he ran behind me and caught my arm.

Afraid to speak I went back to the shop with him and waited while the hand was wrapped. I handed him his white hat and walked out into the late night noise with him, committed for the final tour and the drunken talk until the lights went out and he was deposited on a bed…

The next night coming back on the train he roared and stamped his feet and yelled, "Goddamn slopeheads, goddamn scoop-jaws," and overheated threw up at the feet of a young girl.

At the Sagami Otsuka station, I braced him against me and went down the platform steps and through the ticket gate. The lights had not yet gone out in the town. There was music and women were standing in the doorways.

I led him toward a cab and held the door open. "We've had a rough weekend; we'd better go back to the base."

Fred ducked his head into the taxi and then came out of it. "You know, I think I'll go see Crackerjack at the Clover."

"Why don't you just go on back to the base? I think you've had enough to last a weekend." I forced him back into the cab and seated myself beside him.

"Look, this is none of your goddamn business," he yelled.

The driver turned his head and watched us.

I said "Okay" and backed out of the cab. He went by me with the force of his shoulder against my chest.

The driver yelled, "You want cab?" and I didn't answer.

Two sailors brushed past me and got into the taxi and it clashed past.

My eyes followed him until he turned into the narrow alley that led to the Clover. I may have taken several steps to follow him, but finally I went back to the post in front of the station and leaned against it. I stood waiting for the next cab. A *joson* came out of the San Francisco and looked at me. I said softly "Piss on you," and moved my eyes back to the corner. In a minute around this corner a cab will come.

LETTER TO KAZUKO
C/O BAR DESIRE

This poem was published in the Carolina Quarterly, *Winter 1959*

For the first star
And the final mating
Enclosed find thirty dollars,
Ten thousand and eight hundred yen.
Buy the summer kimono,
The two black sashes
That match the night birds,
The bordering caprice....
When you tie the first sash
That deepens the melon swing,
Remember me;
With the second sash
That girders the fountain,
The overflow, the downward symmetry
Remember me....

Kazuko, I am back in the city.
This is a different country.
I rise in the night
And notice the sea....
The great limbs aching
In the wind....

I am lonely; no one touches me.
The buds of the cherry trees
Are broken now; petal snow
In my window light
Trenches the gutters....
How is the hill?

The travelers there,
The crowfeather hair,
Is it still cut straight
Across their foreheads?
And are they solemn in
Their wooden *geta*,
The school books
And umbrellas?
I have no doubt.
The japonicas we planted
On the fringes of the courtyard
Have they budded?
I question too much....

It is late, too late;
A roommate mumbles toward
My light, turning...
Blossoms, petal swirling....

Chodai, I ask you,
Send me love.
Chodai, I ask you,
Send me love.

EXCERPTS FROM THE JOURNAL OF A SAD, FAT WORDMAN

> "Imprisoned in every fat man a thin one is wildly signaling to be let out." *The Unquiet Grave*, Cyrus Connolly

7/30/60

Two lightening bugs are courting against my window screen. Their tail lights flickering. I think that is what they are doing. Courting. It is hard to be sure because they are visible only in the distorted micro-flashes. If I wait long enough, if I sit patient, maybe I will see a difference, the slow lighted pulse of post coitum tristesse. Apart, no longer lighting the screen and themselves. If I am patient.

It is not that I am interested in the sex life of bugs. No. Not like the school children pressed against the second story window watching the two dogs next to the Confederate monument. It is not that I lack curiosity, either. No. I remember once stopping halfway through Krafft-Ebing. I think it was when I read about the French farmer who kept the handkerchief wadded up in his armpit for weeks, not taking it out all through the harvest. And at the dance after the harvest had only to wipe a girl's sweaty brow with it to excite and seduce her. I think this case history showed me how shallow my own life is. Since I insist on using underarm deodorant even when my armpits are full of infected glands. Caused by the creams, the sticks, the squeeze bottles.

I think I realized that while I was outwardly satisfied to be an outcast, a forty year old man living in a basement, I was really trying to slip in the backdoor by proving to everyone that my armpits smelled as good as theirs. My secret fantasy was that people would comment upon my effort not to offend in the same subdued and bland way that toilet tissue is advertised on t.v. It would have meant a lot to me. To be noticed. As it is now, now that I realize that this attempt to conform has been taken by these people as something I owed them, as their just due, I am left with what is probably, outside of a drug store, the best stock of underarm deodorants in town. And when I last counted ten swollen, inflamed glands under my right arm and fourteen under my left. It is so painful that I have to buy my shirts three sizes too large. It seems to be a circle. Several times, a bit proud of how I smell, I go to a bar and drink a beer, elated, my shoulders squared, my stomach pulled in, only to notice after a time that the other people are looking at my shirts in the same way that people look at used clothing at a Junior League Rummage Sale. It must be a circle.

But the lightening bugs. I noticed them first out of the corner of my eye as I sat at my desk doing the final draft of my juvenile novel. I thought at first they were headlights, that Fanny had changed her mind and come by for a drink. But no, it is only the molting season for lightening bugs. I returned to my desk and rewrote another ten pages.

My agent has said that she feels that my forte is the juvenile novel, that I am just enough out of touch with the street gangs and the prepuberty sex clubs to exert the kind of influence on young minds that the PTA approves of. Of course she does not think that my title, *The Ratsuck Boys in Peace and War*, is as effective as it might be. Not enough wham in it. Even if, she argues, the family in the novel is the Ratsuck family do I really feel that Ratsuck has the eye appeal that will increase the sales? Will little boys and girls secretly wish to belong to the family? Will it become a household word like Swift? Like Jack Armstrong? I have no answer yet. It is up to the children, bless them.

Now I have to stop for the day. It is midnight and Fanny is not coming and it is time to walk across town to the A&P and see what the big truck left outside tonight. Last night they left only fifty pound bags of peat moss and I had nothing to eat all day. If I were only a flower.

7/31/60

I checked the post office box at 7 am and found that I had received my 23rd rejection on my adult novel, *Son of Lesbia, Brother to Catullus*. The envelope has my agent's address on it, but there is nothing inside but the rejection from Doubledare. Perhaps she is giving up. I do not see why. For example, this is the best rejection I have received in the last six months. Just the length of the letter makes me want to go out and buy two or three of their latest best sellers.

It makes you believe in big companies.

Doubledare Publishers
415 Mad. Ave.
New York, New York

Dear Writer,
It is with a great and profound regret that we find that we must inform you that we have no place in our list for your (underscore one: novel, play, verse, travel, biography, other). We particularly regret this because we feel that you have talent. Over the years we have found that it is disturbing to both the writer and the publisher to offer to the public a book which does not sell well enough to justify our faith. So that you will know that we have seriously considered your work, we are enclosing our interpretation of several of the readers' reports.

A reading by three homosexuals in the mail room has assured us that there is not enough homosexual material in the novel for us to feel that we could effectively slant our sales approach toward them. Over the years, we have found that this rather disorganized group buys at least twenty thousand copies of any book dealing kindly with them.

Our women's expert has given the book a close reading and believes that the great mass of women who frequent the lending libraries will not be critically appreciative. She feels that the scene where Mrs. Dubose is seduced by the one-armed gardener was your best chance to interest them. That you are unwilling to do the scene completely and retreat to a five page account of how a ripe near falls from a tree nearby and is eaten by a swarm of flies she finds neither artistic nor brave.

Mr. Freund, the church editor, finds there is not enough sadomasochistic material to interest the Bible Book Club. As you know our study, *The Agony of Christ*, a detailed account of all the possible pains and tortures of Christ on the Cross, documented by two years of study and medical experimentation on dogs and apes and fully illustrated with color plates of automobile accidents and knifings, is now in the fifteenth printing and is number one on the *New York Times* best seller list.

Our literary editor who teaches at N.Y.U. and spends only Thursday afternoons with us believes that this is the best novel since *Madame Bovary*. Unfortunately, our figures on the sale of *Madame Bovary* during the past year (1,344. copies) do not encourage us to consider his opinion any longer than we have to.

Our regrets once more.
Sincerely,
underscore one: (Blake, Watson, Wilson)

I was not always this way. I was not always a walking earthworm, a grub. Not at all. When I was a child my mother, wanted me to be a Methodist preacher and my father wanted me to be a left-handed pitcher. I became neither of these, but it shows that they wanted something normal for me, they wanted me to fit in. For my father, the sickness began when I fell down a grease pit at the corner service station and broke my right arm. Until then I am not sure that he had noticed me. Now, suddenly, he saw me eating with my left hand. It set him off.

He bought me a Lefty Gomez autographed glove and I had to spend two hours each afternoon pitching into his Bill Dickey autographed catcher's mitt. He never gave up. Even after the cast was removed from my right arm. After two years I was still, in a town full of stuttering left-handed children, the only one who could not be right-handed if he wanted to.

My mother, poor, frail southern lady that the was loved God and me and Methodism all in the same breath. As the years passed, it seemed that God was not the cure but the habit. She was too dignified to argue with my father: as far as I know she never even called him by his first name. Also, she was too much a lady not to want what my father wanted. It is almost as if she believed that I could belong to the New York Yankees four months a year and to God the other eight without having any contractual troubles. Only December 1941 and the war saved me from God and the New York Yankees.

I was in a tattoo parlor in Honolulu having a six inch black leopard with bloody claws inked into the flesh of my right shoulder that night in the summer of 1943 when she ate a whole tiger watermelon and died on the front porch because she could not stop burping.

Note: When I went by the A&P I found that I would have nothing to eat for another day. I found only cases of Dial Soap and twenty-five pound bags of sheep manure. On my first trip, I brought away two cases of Dial Soap: Dial should cure the ulcers under my arms, if no other way by making the hair fall out as it has done with the hair on my head.

The second trip I brought back a hundred pounds of sheep manure which I poured around the roots of a young peach tree in my yard. Perhaps I was hasty, perhaps four bags of manure is more than a young peach tree can stand. I thought about it during the night and I meant to go out early this morning and shovel away two-thirds of it. As soon as I stepped outside I realized that it had rained during the early hours of the morning and the sheep manure had soaked far down into the earth and the hidden roots. Now I will have to hope for the best. It would be too much if I did harm while trying to do good. Poor young peach tree.

8/5/60

Fanny did come last night. I had planned all afternoon what I would say to her. I washed the two jelly glasses and dusted off the cognac bottle. As an afterthought I went into the garden of the lady next door and stole sane roses, a heavy armful of dew wet red roses. In the excitement, I did not realize that I had nothing to put the roses in, that I usually pretended the jelly glasses were vases and now the glasses were on display with the cognac bottle. Finally I tacked the roses up around the door and the windows in little bunches. There was nothing else I could do with them.

Fanny. She came at nine when I was about to give her up. I met her at the door with the candle and led her to my room with the sweet harshness of the jasmine she wore all around me. It was to be a candlelight meeting. I had told her on the phone the night before because I wanted to be sure that she would not be surprised or offended.

I am not always this shy with her. Sometimes I am rather bold. Perhaps what hinders me is that I am not sure why she continues to see me. What does she see in me that no one else sees?

Once, late at night after seeing her, I thought I had the explanation. The old saw: that a man should have a brilliant wife to talk to and a beautiful mistress for his bed. It seemed right, it seemed possible. I believed it for a whole day from the moment I crawled out of bed at seven o'clock until long after midnight when I returned from the A&P. Believing it, so happy I could choke. Until I stretched out on the bed and said to myself, "Empty out," and all the stray thoughts and events of the day paraded across my dark mind like leaf shadows against a window, moving quickly, tumbling over each other ... and out my left ear. But near the end, when they were smaller and quieter, when I was rolling over to put my face in the pillow I heard the lion part of me that will not lie say," Who ever told you that you were brilliant?"

And ruined it completely.

About Fanny, so that I will not forget. Something might happen and I might want to remember everything about her. She is taller than I am, perhaps even five inches taller. And slender to a painful degree. It may be that this is her most attractive aspect. It is almost as if she is only skin and bones, the skin so closely layered over the bones that often, then the light touches her squarely, a bluish tinge radiates from her. Her hair is blond and rather coarse, that color I have spoken of as weathered corn tassle. Under my hand when I touch it, shyly, furtively, it is often damp, as if she has just come from the bath. The color of her eyes? I cannot think of a time when I have looked directly into her eyes. I have always found it difficult to correctly judge the eye color from the side. I will find out the next time I see her. If nothing else I will ask her. I do not think she will mind if I ask.

Last night. I put the candle on the table just beyond the glasses and the bottle. First of all, as I always do, I lifted one of the glasses and the bottle and asked if she would like some cognac. As always she said that she had just had a drink before she left her apartment. She said that she would wait. I put the bottle and the glass aside and said that I would wait with her. Was that too bold? Will she think I meant anything by it? At the time it meant nothing to me, I said it without thinking. I noticed no reaction. But there is the chance that she reflected upon it later. I will have to be more careful.

We talked about literature. Last night I think we talked about Jane Austen. As far as I know, Fanny has never read a book, but she talks very well. As I recall last night, I was making a case for Jane Austen as the best realist, bar none, in our literature. Is it, I remember saying, that the writers today are fascinated by the corpses and the lime trees, the jewels and the mud? Do they represent life as they see it, as it is reflected by the mirror in the roadway or is it some kind of fascination with the distorted, with the real which is not common enough to be real?

Fanny nodded. "You may have something there."

What is life, I shouted, bat the trivial, the continuing boredom, the petty? The horror of birth lulled by the bland diet of life until not even the horror of death worries us?

"Yes," Fanny said, "yes."

If this is true, if life is dull, petty, isn't Jane Austen's concern with getting her young lady married to the man with the most English pounds a year as vital, as worthy (and perhaps even more accurate) as the latest novel about the crazy hitchhiker who kills four people in four different ways? While helping out the author by advancing his plot.

"Yes," Fanny said.

I could tell she was restless. It was the way she rocked her leg, the abrupt way she stubbed out her cigarette in the rim of one of the jelly glasses. She closed her stenographer's pad with a loud smack and clicked her purse shut over it.

"I have to go ," she said, rising.

"Will you come tomorrow?"

She shook her head. "Tomorrow is my party."

"Of course. I'm sorry."

I am embarrassed as if I had asked for an invitation to her party and had been refused. Actually I am only trying to save the trouble of calling her. I know that she is having the party: otherwise she would not come to see me. It is not that I mind her writing in the stenographer's pad. No. At first I wondered about it and I was as afraid as I was flattered. Later I realized that she had been frightened by a Book of the Month Club advertisement and I could not be angry with her: often we have only what the newspapers, magazines, and the TV lets us have.

It has interested me how she has changed: two months ago she would have been disappointed by my remarks about Jane Austen. She would have taken out her list of bestsellers and asked me to comment on one or two of them. Now, she has found that her guests consider her interest in Jane Austen, Henry James, Flaubert, Zola and others much superior to their reading of the latest novel about the stage struck girl from Iowa who goes to New York, is seduced and brutalized by a pimp, and travels twice the length of the country with a group of girls and a white slaver who beats them with a whip, but lives to marry the head of the Mafia and settle down in a $100,000 ranch-style house in Bucks County. Of course, the guests all say, Jane Austen is not as interesting.

Often, before Fanny leaves, she flips back through her notebook and reads out a line or two. "Is that what you said?" If my mind moves fast enough, I can change a word here and there, a verb which is not sharp enough, strike out an adjective... but last night she seemed satisfied. It was as if we had played the game so long that I had won without even trying.

I lighted the way to the outside door with the sputtering candle. The jasmine scent trailed her down the long damp hall, leaving with her, unwilling to stay. I watched her turn out of the driveway and hurried back to the room to search for the cigarettes she always "loses" at some out of the way place. It is a matter of pride that I will accept only one cigarette from her. I would not take a full pack if the offered them. So we have developed this ritual: when I offer her cognac from the empty bottle, she refuses it kindly and when she leaves the cigarettes, I smoke then only because I know they will become stale before she comes back.

I am too tired to walk to the A&P.

8/7/60

Bread, spring onions and pithy carrots and a heavy rainfall at the A&P. A picture of Fanny and the Governor on the society page of the *Morning Herald*. The caption underneath says "Admirers of Jane Austen confer at $100-a-plate luncheon."

8/10/60

Years ago, someone asked me why I had settled in Chapel Hill. I was not able to answer. I have a difficult time getting people to like me. It does no good to offend them. It would not have helped me at all.

I think I charged the subject. I could not tell him about the corpse and the lime trees. In one of Gustave Flaubert's journals there is an account of a trip he and Ducamp take through Egypt, Asia, Greece and Italy. At one place, coming toward a town, they pass through a lime orchard where a thief had been hung several days before and is still hanging. The two warring scents, both with an essence of sweetness in them, have become a signpost for modern writers.

"Interesting," my friend would have said," but what does that have to do with …?"

Opposites, I would have said, a kind of attitude I like. An atmosphere so sterile I could create within it.

"But which are you," he would ask," the corpse or the lime trees?"

The corpse, I think.

9/1/60

No. Yesterday I found the quotation from the journals of Flaubert. Quote: "That reminds me of Jaffa, where as we approached the town I smelled at the same moment the odor of lemon-trees and that of corpses; half-crumbled skeletons lay about in the caved-in cemetery, while over our heads golden fruit hung from green branches. Don't you feel the consummate poetry of this, that it is the grandest possible synthesis?"

Yes, Mr. Flaubert, the agriculture show and the love words on the balcony. Yes.

But my lime trees and my thief are as true ... perhaps truer.

9/5/60

Today I remember what it was that, more than my father and mother, pointed me toward this basement. It is that I want to be liked by people I do not like. Can I explain this? You will not understand even if I do.

Seven years ago. It was a picture I saw seven years ago. I was in Japan, at the transient barracks at Yokusuka. Headed back for the States. I was sitting on my bunk, smoking, watching the night come on. Across a narrow aisle from me, another sailor was packing his seabag, all his junk spread out on the mattress cover. A picture slid from his bed and floated to the floor between my feet. I leaned down to pick it up and hand it back. But stopped to look at it.

At first I was not sure what it was. I saw the background, the Japanese houses dark and weathered to the color of driftwood, and then holding it toward the last afternoon light, I saw three faces. Two were sailors, grinning, smiling into the camera, showing their all-American teeth. The other face was that of a young Japanese girl, her mouth open, screaming, her eyes rolled back. I looked at the full picture and understood it: two sailors are holding a girl, one sailor's hand pulling the sweater and torn bra up around her neck so that the full dark-tipped breasts were bare, while another

sailor snaps the shutter. The girl's face. The scream. All human dignity gone. The
> scream I can hear.

"Nice, huh?" the sailor asked, grinning the two sailors' grins when I handed the picture back to him. I agreed that it was.

9-7-60

This morning when I went to the window I saw a robin flying around and around the young peach tree. As if trying to decide whether the tree was real or a stage prop made of papier-mache.

At a distance, the tree appeared to be the same as ever. But closer, I touched one of the leaves which are usually crisp and waxy and found that was soft and withered. It felt like a doeskin glove. Leaf after leaf I went around the tree, touching, holding. All withered, all dying. For a time, while I watched the robin continued to circle around the tree and around me, at ever increasing distance, until finally he flew past a hedge and out of sight.

RETURN OF THE SAD, FAT ORGANIZATION MAN

"We are now in great haste to construct a magnetic telegraph from Maine to Texas; but Maine and Texas, it may be, have nothing important to communicate." *Thoreau*

12/31/61

Winter now. The last day of the year. The first snow of this winter is piled high against my narrow basement window and the last flakes fell only an hour ago. A dirty green light from a bug repellant someone left burning last summer smears the yard and the grave-shaped hump where the young peach tree was once, where I dug around the roots from time to time to give them space to grow. And watched it, without ever bearing fruit, wither and turn as black and fragile as a completely burnt matchstick. The way as children my girlfriend, Wilma, and I used to burn with special care a match from end to end to see if it would crook... the crook meaning that my wife or her husband would have a crooked back. Wilma.... the last time I saw her, she was hanging still lightly soiled diapers on a backyard clothes line.

A few minutes ago, I went out into the hallway and walked to the outside door. Why, I forget. Perhaps to see if there was a moon. But I saw instead the path to my door, bordered by twisted stumps that would be spring bushes, and covered with three inches of smooth undisturbed snow. For only a moment, for the time it took me to step back and close the door, it seemed to have some meaning for me. The well-laid out path to my door with no footprints on it. But as I have done before, many times before, as I felt the meaning begin to find its subject and verb I squeezed it in my hand until I heard it splatter against the walls.

And went back to work on my new book, *A Child's History of Autoeroticism.*

Though it is quiet, I am not alone. I have company. A field mouse lives in my room during the winter … in the room or in the hall outside. He does not completely trust me, but we do have some rapport. Late at night, the lights out, when he wants to leave my room and go out into the hallway he scratches at my door until I say, "Alright," and then hides behind the bookcase. I open the door for him, wait five minutes and then close it once more. He is always a perfect gentleman and never wakes me more than once a night.

1/1/62

The New Year. I am older now and even in the middle of this end I have much of my beginning. The hour glass is running down, but it is the same sand that marks this hour from midnight to one a.m. that told us it was two-thirty yesterday afternoon. And will tell us when it is three o'clock tomorrow morning. In fanciful moments, when I think of it at all, I like to believe that the sand is made up of the bitter centers of Carter's Little Liver Pills.

My New Year resolution. I will put on pretty yellow wings and fly. And no longer be a bug, a maggot, the rotting body of a fly that has not yet been issued wings. Green as things that grow under rocks. Wide yellow wings with blue things painted on.

For the Governor, on Christmas eve, loving Jane Austen and high culture and the sweeter-the-meat-the-thinner-the-bone, married Fanny during the seventh inning stretch at the Watch Jesus Get Born service at the purple painted chapel of the Church of God. And carried her across the threshold of the Executive Mansion just at one minute past twelve while the photographers from *Life, Look, Time* and *Fortune* elbowed each other and cursed and knelt to sight the two inch swagger of her French Lace petticoat.

And I found that it was no longer worthwhile loving art. My Gland, the one that writers and painters and poets have and that the medical textbooks do not list or describe but is shaped like a plasma bottle with a sixteen inch plastic tube attached, instead of the one drop of gall and doubt gave me eight yesterday and sixteen already today. Tomorrow, thirty-two if it increases at the same rate.

I do not really blame Fanny. The hurry before the skin tone goes is something her mother taught her. Made her write fifty times in her copybook before she was fifteen. The copybook... I saw it once. She brought it to me one Fall afternoon some months ago and put it into my hands with all the reverence that one must use in handling a Sliver of The Cross and said that this was her soul and if I read it I would know her better than even a husband might. A sacred trust, she called it. Which so moved and frightened me that I washed my hands and cleaned my fingernails before I opened it.

On page one, in the raw, undigested Palmer Method hand, copied 37 times:

I must carry myself today and everyday as if the jewel of myself and all my womanhood was locked in a chest that only the key of love can open, (and in the margin: must ask Miss Riffsynder at B.T.U. what this means.)

On page two:
A woman without virtue is like a ship without rudder.

On page eight:
Rules: be intelligent, be beautiful, be clean and do not laugh at dirty jokes (and crossed out, but still readable under the stroke of the penstaff) *even if they are funny.*

On page twelve:
Tonight, on the way back from B.T.U. Billy Bronson kissed me and did not seem to know how much I had given him.

1/3/62

A poem I wrote for the season.
> Quite contrary the wind weds Mary
> In gardens where stalkers grow,
> And Lust, when brick walls fail
> Supports six rapists in a row.

This morning, very early, before the streets were crowded, I walked downtown to leave my suit to be cleaned of its green and mold and shine. On my, way back I stopped off and had my hair cut by an old man with arthritic hands and a punctual stomach growl.

These are not everyday actions and I will have to explain. But not now. The idea is too new, the plot fantastic, and I will have to chew it up into a fine mash and swallow it before I can vomit it up again with any kind of sanity. But not now. Tomorrow, if it does not rain, I will walk downtown at noon into the loud swarm of students and towns-people and prepare myself, become accustomed. I will swim into that sea and undertow of armpits and pretend that I am as good as any two of them.

1/4/62

Last night when I went by the A&P at the usual time the truck was late and since it was a fine, clear night I waited back in the shadows until it came. I was so sure that I was out of sight that I was surprised when the driver swung the rear doors open and said, without looking in my direction, "Hey, give us a hand here." And I did, standing on the platform while he handed out the trays of bread that smelled of wax and sawdust and the pound cakes with the characteristic scent of sugar and synthetic rubber. When it was done he leaped out of the hellmouth of the truck with a loaf of bread in one hand and a crushed pound cake in the other. He presented them to me with an awkward flourish like a courtly bow and would not let me thank him.

Walking home, the bread and the cake carried openly, framing my answer if the police car stopped me, polishing it, honing it, I began to realize that there is a certain amount of Horatio C. Alger in us all.

1/5/62

This morning when I went to the cleaner's to get my suit I saw Benji Hufflefinger. In another time, another age, Dr. Bovary would have operated on his clubfoot... if he had one. And made him really lame. But now, in a society where even the village idiot is not allowed to be a drone or a parasite, Benji has been made useful. Every morning, when it is just bare light, if you notice, you will see him collecting the pennies from the parking meters. Pushing the little cart with two wheels and a heavy canvas sack hanging down in front like testicles. He is short, crablike, with a neck as thick as a tree, and a flattened nose which, at a distance, makes it appear that he has either four eyes or three mouths. That is, until you are close to him and you realize that his nostrils, the openings the size of half dollars, are as flat against the spade of his face as his mouth or his eyes.

In many ways, when I think of Benji at all, I believe in him as a Saint, as a Jesus type. The kindness, the gentleness and the childlike quality.

Once, several years ago, exactly when I have forgotten, like I forget the deposits on yesterday's dirty handkerchief, two policemen decided that Benji was missing something out of life (wink and snigger, snigger) and took him to a carnival and fixed him up with one of the show girls, paying for it out of their own money. And waited outside the trailer until Benji ran out screaming, and had their laugh which was worth the ten dollars. Benji's brother, Abraham, who had his position in the Bank to consider, heard about it a day later and thought about putting him in Butner. Afraid because now that Benji knew what a woman was he might become a sex maniac and no woman in town would be safe. For weeks he went to bed expecting his telephone to ring. Any night. Every night. But he might have saved himself the ulcer. The morning after the visit to the carnival, at the police station the jokes got cruder and rawer and rawer while Benji adjusted his dirty white cowboy hat over his eyes like Matt Dillon did and tried to remember.... tried to understand....

1/6/62

The suit is too large now, the pleats in the trousers a darker color than the rest of the suit and the one-button roll of the jacket bothers me. But perhaps it will do for the interview. If I can manage to keep my topcoat on.

Last night I left for the A&P early and waited in the cold for twenty minutes to see of the same driver would come. It was his night off and the relief was a nice man named Charlie Brunnie who is not married and talked a lot about the girls he knew, grunting their names as he handed the crates of wilted carrots out to me. In fine detail about what great *bods* they all have. It is amazing that one man could know so many girls with great *bods* on them. But not impossible. Before he left we smoked a cigarette in the doorway, out of the wind. After a couple of puffs he threw his into a snowbank, where it hissed. I got to move on, he said, hand on my shoulder, but sometime we ought to get together on my night off and see a couple of girls. This one named Sadie knows a thing or two and you can bet on that.

On the way home, stopping now and then to clean a carrot in the snow before I ate it, I imagined a girl named Sadie from head to toe who it must be admitted looked quite a bit like Fanny and had a great *bod* on her.

1/7/62

The interview is with a man from B.B.D. and O. A friend of Fanny's. Or rather a friend of the Governor's wife. This is, in her words, a last attempt to salvage something out of my life. Thirty-eight and balding, she insists, is not too old to start over. Not if I have ambition.

Mr. Criscoomb is not coming to Chapel Hill to see me. I doubt that he would come this far without a better reason. No. He is the headline speaker at the Symposium. The theme this year is *What Young America Wants to Know*. His topic, on the third evening, is *How to Obtain Employment in an Advertising Agency During these Decisive Days of Radioactive Babies and Revolt in the Congo*. The latter part of his speech will be a fashion show on what to wear and how to wear it and how often is a haircut necessary and the importance of keeping the nostril hairs trimmed. At the special question and answer session afterwards he will, if prompted, advise the young students on whether to button the button in back of the shirt collar, or is that trying too hard? The next day, at private conferences, if the interested young students will bring their girlfriends to meet him, he has offered to interview them and decide whether they will make good wives for executives.

Why am I driven to this point? I would have never considered it a year ago. Nothing could have made me. Perhaps it is this: Some kind of awareness that in the cold and damp basement I am not really hatching a revolution from underneath ... but only living in a cold and damp basement. Rousseau, in his exhibitionism before the milkmaids, is my bad-tempered brother. So that, when no one will come by, even to pick my brain, it is time to start over. And perhaps if I can really decide once and for all and not turn to salt, the 1024 drops will go away.

In my life I have done six novels:

The Ratsuck Boys in Peace and War. 237 pages.
Son of Lesbia, Brother to Catullus. 498 pages.
Affairs of the Tattooed Lady. 345 pages.
King of Doughnuts. 765 pages.
From Here to Anywhere. 455 pages.
The Last First Time.. 301 pages.

And published none of them. And today I stopped work on *A Child's History of Autoeroticism* on page 299.

1/10/62

"…in a word, they put the Real in the place of the Ideal." De Tocqueville

Several months ago, a little magazine of the arts here in town ran four pages of photographs of manhole covers. Beautiful, real manhole covers. The best looking manhole covers I have ever seen. But after all, when all the shouting is done, only Real manhole covers. Not one picture of an Ideal manhole cover. For, even if, by careful laboratory work, one manhole cover was made out of six or even ten photographed ones, it would still be a Real manhole cover. And that is the way the world is: not one Ideal Manhole cover for people who love beauty.

1/11/62

The interview is today. In Mr. Criscoomb's suite at the Carolina Inn. Last night, when I was out walking in the snow, Fanny came by to see me and left one of the Governor's old neckties on the off or certain chance that I would not have one. In the closed-off, airless basement so much of her scent remained that I vomited, out of pain and love, in the corner of the room. All day, waiting for two o'clock, I have been trying to create an advertising campaign with which I could surprise Mr. Criscoomb. All I can remember is F. Scott Fitzgerald's slogan for a steam laundry in Muscatine, Iowa: "We keep you clean in Muscatine" to which his boss at the Barton Collier agency is supposed to have said that it was a bit too imaginative but if he stayed at the agency he would probably learn better. I considered attempting to impress Mr. Criscoomb with a variation of his slogan. And decided against it because it might be a classic in its field. Or even worse it might be that B.B.D. and O do not handle accounts for steam laundry advertising anymore.

One-forty-five and I have dressed and I am wearing the Governor's tie for luck. The kidney-shaped tomato juice stain looks hand painted in Paris.

Now it is time to go. There is not time to worry about it anymore. If it happens it happens.

Lord of Little Children, Watch over me.

Tolstoi, Watch over me.

Stendal, Write me a Letter.

Gertrude Stein, Goodbye.

"Although Dennis wrote his *Sad Fat Wordman* off the top of his head at first, he has become rather attached to him. 'I would like to believe in the Sad Fat Wordman, but not too deeply. Some of the local artists had believed in him – he was sort of the man living in the garret. They identified with him. Then when I did the second story, when he began to sell out, they didn't like him anymore. I'm going to try to win them back with the third story.'

Dennis describes the Wordman as an unhappy soul who somehow remains fat although skirting the brink of starvation; he lives off what he can find outside of the freight doors of the local A&P by the night delivery men.

On good nights, he dines well; other times the shipment may be an inordinate amount of sheep manure intended for local lawns. His production of literature consists of improbably titles on a widely and wildly improbable series of themes.

There is a faint autobiographical note here, to the extent that Dennis has pulled a couple of hitches in Chapel Hill garrets and basements while working and writing. 'There are basements and garrets in Chapel Hill, but my wife won't let me live in them anymore.'"

— from *The Chapel Hill Weekly,* August 1, 1963, in an article entitled *Dennis Plans Year of Study at Yale.*

THE SON OF THE SAD, FAT WORDMAN GOES NORTH

"For instance, Blankbin, the nun, was constantly tormented by the thought of what could have become of that part of Christ which was removed in circumcision." Psychopathia Sexualis

"The modern tragic hero is a man committed to something which he knows in his own heart to be absurd." Life, Art and Tragedy, *Abraham Burgess*

2/1/62
This afternoon...late afternoon...I married Miss Clarissa Vauxhall Hedgefox in an empty Baptist church just off Franklin Street. A cold rainy Chapel Hill day with the bare dark trees slick with a sugary thin ice. And the coeds walking up and down the street, while Clarissa and I waited under the colonial portico of the church for Reverend Sandwich to arrive, had legs that were roast beef pink with razor burn. Clarissa, huddled against my soaked raincoat, said, "In a few minutes it will be against the law for you to look at other girls." And smiled.

I, with a rare show of wit, blew on her glasses until they fogged and asked, "What other girls?"

To be exact, the church was not empty. There were two witnesses as the law requires. Or is it God? One we had not planned upon, a Mrs. Lelia Earp, was in the church already, in answer to the sign on the church lawn, PRAY AGAINST THE BOMB 9-5, and stayed at our request, crying throughout the service with all the energy and pride of a professional mourner. The second witness was Clarissa's mother, Edna Vauxhall Hedgefox, a thin stately Southern lady who looks at the world through the venom of a single eye, the empty socket of the other eye covered by a white satin eyepatch trimmed with black sequins. Clarissa told me a few days ago, with a certain misplaced glee, that her mother lost the eye on the day Clarissa was conceived: on a hot August noon while her mother and father waited for the tea to steep, on a bed where minutes before the mother had been crocheting lace doilies. It was, according to Clarissa, the high point in their connubial bliss... before it vanished forever.

The Reverend Arthur Sandwich. Think of teeth the color and texture of blue cheese. A nose the shape and hue of a dry gourd. A Phi Beta Kappa key worn purposely upside down as a tie clasp. A dogeared copy of *Fear and Trembling* sticking out of his right suitcoat pocket. And a voice that rattled about in the dry gourd nose, the words like so many seeds, so that I, wanting to treasure every moment of the ceremony, heard none of it.

On the way down the steps, afterwards, Clarissa and I dodged the fluttering scraps of a letter Mrs. Earp threw at us in place of rice, while she shouted, "Have a lot of strong healthy children with good bones."

At the bottom step, I turned to catch a scrap of paper, just in time to hear Edna Vauxhall Hedgefox say to the Reverend Sandwich: "Mark my words. The first child is going to be born a little long in the teeth."

Which puzzled me until Clarissa explained to me on our wet bridal march to my basement that long teeth are an inherited trait from the Vauxhall side of the family.

It was a whirlwind courtship. Even Clarissa, who is more romantic than I am because she is a woman, could not get over how surprising it was. I had only known her 18 days, having met her for the first time on the afternoon I kept my appointment with Mr. Criscoomb of B.B.D. and O at the Carolina Inn.

FROM THE JOURNAL ENTRY THAT DAY:

1/11/62 EVENING

Mr. Criscoomb and I faced each other across a low narrow table, while a younger man, Mr. Browninhouser, sat behind me and to my right taking notes in an ornate leather clipboard. I am not certain how well I did. It is hard, looking back on the hour, to establish any kind of rules that might help in a judgement of success or failure. But there was one problem, a moment when

I failed in the interview protocol. The lighter I had found on the street a week before and had displayed proudly just before we were seated…suddenly gave out of fluid and I had brought no matches. Still, doggedly, each time Mr. Criscoomb offered me a cigarette from his silver case I whipped out my lighter and grind, grind, grind…sparks but no flame. Behind me, the chair squeaked as Mr. Browninhouser leaned forward to register a notation on his clipboard. Each time it sounded like a small ordinary "x". After Mr. Criscoomb had lit our cigarettes for the second time, he leaned back in his chair and burped delicately.

"For your personal file," he said.

"Age?"

"Thirty-six."

"Occupation?"

"Writer."

"Weight?"

"Two hundred and forty-seven."

"Height?"

"Five-feet-ten."

"And…" Mr. Criscoomb looked beyond me at the gray winter afternoon, "…and under Other Physical Remarks balding."

Mr. Browninhouser's pen scratched out *b-a-l-d* and stopped. Only when I turned in my chair to look at him did he lift his pen once more and add *i-n-g*.

"Advertising experience?"

"None."

"Publication?"

"None."

"College degrees and honorary societies?"

"None."

"Civic club memberships?"

"None."

"Page three." And after Mr. Browninhouser had turned two pages: "Why do you want to work for B.B.D. and O?"

"Because you have the best advertising agency in the world."

Mr. Criscoomb leaned forward and shook his head.

"Because I like advertising."

Another shake of his head.

"Because I like New York."

"No, the real reason."

"Because I am tired of living in a basement. Because I am tired of being a failure."

Mr. Criscoomb frowned and Mr. Browninhouser, without making a mark, closed his clipboard with a loud leathery smack.

Like two shoes kissing each other.

Later. A strange and wonderful thing happened to me. In front of the Armpit Cafe, head down, swinging my arms proudly, having decided to make myself somebody, to work my way up to the office of President of B.B.D. and O, I bumped into a girl. My body, the part that touched her, felt like a hand that had pressed an exquisite, ripe plum. Her name, it seems, is Clarissa Hedgefox. A face with the delicate bones of a small child. And hyper-thyroid eyes with the luminous gleam of stars in moving water...Clarissa? I love that part of her at once, because it is the name of my favorite heroine. But the question is: am I her Lovelace?

1/12/62

No letter from Mr. Criscoomb. In the evening it sleeted and I decided not to walk to the A&P to see what the trucks left outside. I might break a leg and I feel I ought to keep myself whole in case I ever see Clarissa again.

A PROSE POEM FOR CLARISSA

In Catholic folklore/ a Saint Teresa pursued by/ the hot hound of a young man,/ but loving only God wrote asking/ what he loved about her, and he replied,/ "Your eyes," plucked them out and sent them/ on a silver platter to him..../ And so, Clarissa, if you loved some part/ of me...my skinny lean heart.../ I would tear it out and send it to you/ by special messenger.

1/13/62

Today I met Clarissa on the street and in the conversation (I'm not sure how it came up) she said she thought I was handsome.

Even the lion part of me that won't lie, that will not leave me one dream, wants to believe it. And I, standing in front of a mirror like an idiot, I knew who stood in front of a mirror and crushed a rose in his right hand and thought, from the reflection, that he crushed the rose in his left hand, say that the reflection lies and

I may, after all, be handsome.

1/28/62

Tonight I asked Clarissa to marry me....

As I remember, she said, "I would like to marry a writer and live in a room full of beautiful words."

I said, "Would you?"

She said, "Yes, I'll marry." And sighed.

2/1/62

The wedding night. Clarissa will not allow me to write about it. I can only say:
1. It was beautiful and holy.
2. She wore a "Vision of Venus" negligee designed by Lili St. Cyr of Hollywood. That it was sheer as a cloud and trimmed with lace.
3. That she does not believe in birth control.
4. That we drank one bottle of champagne.
5. That the object of marriage is to have children.

2/2/62

Today I began a book on Love. My thoughts on love choking me....

To be titled: *Love in a Skinny World.*

Excerpts :

Page 1: "It is not as Plato said, not halves seeking halves, but Wholes and Cripples. Wholes seeking Wholes and Cripples seeking Cripples. A boy I knew who years ago his mother made take toe-dancing (and remained a toe-dancer all his life) married a nice young girl named Emily Dunn and two weeks later his wife ran off with the Bridesmaid... but when Wholes marry Wholes it is different...."

Page 2: "The death of the heart is the beginning of wisdom." Note: I wrote it down as it came off the top of my head (as Mr. Criscoomb might say) and I left it with the hope that it might assume a meaning.

Page 3A: "Married sex... and I can speak of it with some authority, with Clarissa's permission... is the spasmodic death of the heart with the resulting birth of the soul." Note: but what does this birth of the soul have to do with wisdom?

Page 4: A man I know spent twenty years worrying about who he was and what he had to offer a woman If he loved her... until he had only the proof of the twenty years of worry to offer: an ulcer and a diet of baby food. F. Scott Fitzgerald in is his notebooks: "Action is character." What a man does is what he is and what he is is all he can offer. For example: A room full of beautiful words."

2/3/62
We have conceived. Clarissa is certain. A boy. She thinks.

2/6/62
Clarissa saw the doctor today and there is no doubt. Modern methods of detection astound me. Me a father! And Clarissa, knowing more than I do (having counted on nine of my fingers and reached November) tells me that sometimes first children come early, even months early. Which takes, if it happens, some of the worry and waiting out of it.

2/7/62
A light snow as we lay on the bed talking about Jane Austen. A wind that beat against the window like a fist. Then, a moment that I will remember as long as I live. My hand was loose and easy across her plum ripe and grape swollen stomach when suddenly, from inside her, something kicked out at me.

Clarissa saw me jerk my hand away. "Your son," she said and laughing at me, "is talking to you."

All night… awake or half-awake… I waited. Until the alarm clock went off and Clarissa awoke and left for work.

All night… and he'd had nothing more to say.

3/2/62
I tell myself that marriage is a series of experiences. One has to be understanding if one can. This afternoon, I was alone, working on *Love in a Skinny World*, page 163. I was out of paper and needed to write down a thought. The thought: "In South Carolina folklore, there is a belief that ghosts, when they leave their graves, step out of their outer skins, fold them neatly over

the head stones...and then go haunting. The way to get rid of a ghost is to go down to the graveyard and find the right grave stone (and therefore the right outer skin) and salt the inside of the skin. The ghost, returning to the grave just before dawn, steps back into the skin, only to find an agony that he cannot bear. In the same way, the lover has to lose his outer skin and offer himself as a vulnerable being. Only in the trust of his vulnerability can the lover offer himself completely. In the self-protective, the defensive, there is an implied negation."

In the search for paper, I opened a suitcase that belonged to Clarissa. It is not a thing I would usually do. Afterwards I was ashamed...inside, on top, were three used diaphragms and fifty copies of movie magazines, all dealing with different aspects of the Liz Taylor-Richard Burton affair before the marriage. All dog-eared, with pages turned down here and there and passages underlined in red ink.

The sick love, the love out of control, is not what I want. It frightens me to find that Clarissa might have such interests. But she is young and I must try not to wear the outer skin.

I do not understand the three used diaphragms.

4/5/62

The child (my son) seems to have fallen lower. This morning as Clarissa dressed for work I watched her while I pretended sleep. I was reminded of the beauty of a D.H. Lawrence poem about watching his wife, Frieda, taking a sponge bath. "Dijon Roses"?

It is a different beauty...the beauty of the mother-to-be. Both the sexual violence of the wife and the tenderness of the mother-to-be mixed and stirred together. All this beauty for someone who does not, and cannot, deserve it.

7/1/62

I am a father. As of 4:23 this afternoon. A premature boy that weighed ten pounds and three ounces. Clarissa is doing well and the boy is beautiful. Very beautiful: he does not look like either of us.

Clarissa wants to call him Boyd Jay after an uncle on her mother's side of the family. Of course I agreed. There will be other sons to name Henry James, Stendhal, and Sherwood Anderson. Daughters to name Emily Bronte and Jane Austen.

A POEM FOR MY SON
Beautiful Child,
Issue of verbal loins:
The word has a truth that
The picture and the rotten heart
Do not.
Find the right noun,
The proper verb
And the object is always truth.

7/23/62

There is a man always around the house when I come home from work. From the job I've taken washing dishes. I will not let this be salt under my skin. It bothers me that he is always wearing a wet suit and an aqua lung… even if it is not raining outside.

His name is B.J Frankenhiemer. In my least rational moments, when I fight to keep the salt away, I think of him as the bald-headed fish.

Still, I tell myself that a house full of beautiful words might not be enough for a lively girl like Clarissa. The other 20% has to be freedom.

From *Love in a Skinny World*, page 543: "Love is not a trial. Who can be advocates for which side when there is only a middle?"

8/4/62

Clarissa has left me for the scuba diver, B.J Frankenhiemer. When I came home this afternoon I found Boyd Jay in the crib with three bottles of prepared formula carefully stacked beside him.

And a note from Clarissa pinned on a wet diaper which was hanging on the side of the crib.

"*Your love is not enough. Beautiful words suck. The world is full of men and some swim better than others. (You're right: that's a sexual allusion.) Richard Burton is twice the man you are.*"

Liz Taylor

LT/cvh
cc: Boyd J. Frankenhiemer

The cvh leads me to think that she has gone back to her maiden name.

The postscript: "*You're fatfatfatfat...fat. So there*"

At the A&P store, in the Chapel Hill stillness after midnight, a pickup truck unloaded bunches of fresh flowers. Remembering Ezra Pound and his assault on the tulip tree blossoms I ate the petals from a bunch of blue corn flowers so that I could believe that there was something inside of me that was beautiful. And returned home with a gallon of milk and a loaf of warm bread.

Later, stretched out on the bed that was too large for me now, listening to Boyd Jay snore in the crib, emptying my head for the day of camel sized memories that would not go through the eyes of needles, the lion part of me that has only lied once said: "Finish the *Ratsuck* book."

On page 678 of *Love in a Skinny World*, in a shaky Palmer penmanship that would have horrified Miss Emilia Grayson, my sixth grade teacher, I wrote, "It is all a lie."

8/15/62

This morning when I was paid, I offered to work out my two weeks notice. It seemed to be the honorable gesture. The owner. Big Jim Mallard, after looking at Boyd Jay who was asleep on the salad counter with one foot in the lettuce and the other in the chicken salad, said that it was not necessary. It was honorable of me, but not necessary.

At the bus station, with Boyd Jay asleep and bubbling on my shoulder, I told the man at the ticket counter that I was thinking of going somewhere.

"Where?"

Touching my son who must have a good childhood and the best advantages: "Where it snows more than three times a year."

"New York?"

"No." I had heard that the snow in New York is dirty even be? fore it hits the sidewalks.

"Washington? Boston? Cleveland?"

"They don't sound interesting."

A line was forming behind me. "Well, look, when you decide where you want to go…," he broke off as Boyd Jay awoke and turned to look at him. "Where else? Where else?" He seemed to be thinking. "You know, today a kid came in and bought a ticket to New Haven." He leaned across the counter and lowered his voice. "That's where Yale is." A Chapel Hill where it snows more than three times a year?

On the outside chance it might be true I bought the tickets. At the A&P bunches of flowers again. I decided not to eat any of them. It is phony to act like you are beautiful inside when you aren't….

8/16/62

As the bus turned down Franklin Street (settled in for long ride with the diaper pail between my feet) I saw Clarissa and Boyd J. Frankenhiemer standing in front of the Intimate Bookshop. They were both wearing wet suits and aqua lungs. And breathed through snorkels in their rigid mouths. It was not raining at all.

"Wave to your mama, Boyd Jay," I said. "Wave goodbye to your mama." But Boyd Jay, either because he didn't want to look or because he doesn't understand English yet, after a casual look at Clarissa, turned instead and waved at me.

WIND SPRINTS

All things being equal, and this equality being that of disturbed and frightened dreams, it is time to begin. So much garbage in one life and that life only thirty-five years spent. I had not planned to start my autobiography for another twenty-five years. If then. Maybe I'd have waited the full thirty years, for the approaching mellowness, for that one still moment of ripeness before the rot creeps in. No, thunders in, whistles in, explodes upon us. A second consideration: by then, the gall, the bile, might have been thinned down, watered down in the same way that they say the blood of old men is. Waiting, patient, my autobiography might have been charming and whimsical. The reviewers might say: "It brings back an America that doesn't exist any? more." In time, looking back from a distance and blinded by the shapes and shadows of memory, I might have come to believe that my life had its share of charm and beauty. Instead of what it is: a life the parts of which one kicks sand over delicately and moves on, never quite sure later exactly where the lump in the sand really is. Whether I was beaten up by six Japanese policemen in Atsugi or by three bull dykes in San Francisco. Only a few scars over my right eye say that it happened somewhere.

My life to now has been a man's version of what a southern lady's life was once supposed to be. Limited, confined in definition. Born, married, had children, and died.

Born? Check, 1930. In the sandy flat land of South Carolina, in a town called Turbeville. Memories of the violence of both birth and death.

Married? Check, 1960. After the sullen drive down from Chapel Hill until we were across the state line and in South Carolina, in wedlock locked by a J.P. named Angela Slaughter who, in a voice that would have frightened God, asked if we were some of those Chapel Hill reds who believed in integration and that niggers had souls. Be?fore she would sign the marriage certificate we had to assure her that we weren't. Because whatever else we were, finally we were more frightened by the accidental meeting of sperm and egg than we were virtuous about equality.

Had children? Check, one daughter, Evadne. My child in spirit, but never in flesh. The last time I saw Evadne, ugly skinny child with arms and legs knotted like the boles on walking sticks, we were on a beach in Connecticut. Polluted beach. Dead black fish washed up by an oil slick sea. Patterns and swarms of flies. Both walking barefoot on the sand, stepping over the fish. My pale white feet with the sock fuzz still caught under the toenails. Hers bony and tanned, thin and flat as plaster slats. Loving her eye full face, the pale milky blue of marbles. But there was no way of touching her so that she would know and no words that could, with a running start, leap the gap. So that, together, as if by a signal that neither of us had given or had seen, we turned and walked quickly back down the beach to where the car was parked. Disgust and shame, I like to think, in the both of us. But maybe not in her: perhaps relief instead. Squinting into the overcast sky, still and patient while I brushed the sand from her feet with my handkerchief. Evadne was a polite child to the last.

"Come and see me again. Daddy," she said. And I, polite also, said that I would ... soon. A lie between us that calmed the fear we might meet again. That was a year ago, a bit longer, and I have not seen her. Nor does she, I expect, lean on her window sill and wait. Instead, if she leans at her window at all, it is to blow her liquid breath against the cold panes and cloud out any possibility that she will see me.

Divorced? Check, 1964. Not a part of the southern lady's life, but a part of mine. Knowing each other too well, and boredom with what we knew. The chancre in that special rose.

Died? Left blank, not yet. But sometimes I think my whole shabby and discolored life is one prolonged wind sprint toward the grave. (But this is only a heightened sense of melodrama and rhetoric. The other night, parting for the last time from April I said, "All my love be? fore I kick it to death." Knowing quite well that, if one doesn't know what the animal is or where it lives, one has a bit of trouble kicking it to death.) No, I do no wind sprints. My tired body does its own kind of hobbling on. My teeth are bad... in the last two or three months I've noticed they seem to be loosening, maybe even getting out of line so the uppers and lowers don't match anymore. My hair, almost gone, is grown long on the sides and combed across to cover the bare dome center. The small blood vessels in my face appear to be exploding even as I stand in front of the mirror shaving.

The real problem is genitalia. Oh, not that I've lost the ability to make love. On the contrary. One lady rising shakily from my bed, seen through gritty and swollen eyes of a five o'clock dawn, searching for last night's drink, said, "I thought all the great lovers had left town."

I, for want of a better thing to say, answered, "I just got back to town."

"Stay awhile then," she said, "and welcome back."

And I, polite again, said, "Thank you," while another part of me said, "Go home."

Two nights ago, at April's apartment, angry at her because she suddenly moved toward the edge of the bed and said that she was hungry... out of anger I made love to her like I think rape must be. Violating my whole sense of myself and my sense of her. In the breath guttering, the afterwards, I found that I was crying out of this same anger, out of frustration, out of shame that I had found the rapist inside me. I had to hide it, pushing my face into the pillow and blotting against the pillow case... but perhaps a drop fell on her shoulder. At least, she noticed.

"I know why you're crying."

I asked why.

"Because it was so beautiful."

Which made me wonder.

I don't know what has happened. Something has. Maybe as recently as the last two or three months. A loss of soul, a death of the spirit. Or, because words mean nothing, a loss of spirit, a death of then- soul. High and serious terms for this special malaise. I have trouble with words now. I am not a professional writer. I am beyond all hope of that now. In fact, the whole effort to mend my bridges, to protect myself in case the writing came to nothing, has provided me with a good job here at the University. Teaching theater history. "Describe Hanswurst's costume in detail. What were Goethe's rules for action? W. B. Yeat's attitude toward Ibsen and what does it mean?"

The dissertation started and put aside has yet to be done. The students with their basic understanding of what flattery really is call me Doctor. I do not correct them because it takes time away from the class when other more important matters have to be treated, and, I sometimes think, it would be unkind to embarrass them. The notes on the sociological aspects of medieval French drama fade in my carefully kept and carefully avoided filing cabinet. Until the sap and energy rise again.

April. Nymph. Between eighteen and nineteen years old. Strange to picture myself beside her pale blonde image. Last Saturday, at the football game with her, pushing past knees toward our seats, I heard one of the co-eds we passed say, "He must be her father." I looked at April to see if she'd heard and found that she was blushing.

I guess I am her father, both of us loving the scent of ritual incest. The green rank scent of it. Acting out in gesture and a language neither of us understands the closet drama in which the surface is more important than the depths. Once, trying to explain this to her, I said that I was writing my own Poetics. "The modem tragic hero is a man committed to something which he knows in his own heart to be absurd."

"What is absurd?" she asked. Incest and oatmeal cookies.

After a moment: "You haven't answered me."

I know.

"I guess you're not going to answer me."

Pouting. A muscle coils in her back. Ending in the rigid little toe of her left foot. On the side of which there is the centerless pit of a corn.

Words bubble, child, but there is no answer.

"Sometimes I don't think you appreciate my intelligence."

"It is your mind I love most," I say.

The muscle uncoils and the corn disappears under the twisted edge of the sheet. "Daddy you been on my mind," April whispers. A smile which I answer. Then, dully, outside my window, the sharp crack of acorns falling upon unraked leaves. The crack of ice or sleet.

"Child..." I say, now that she is under my wing, her nose wrinkling against the gracing hair of my chest... "Child, winter is not only coming. It is here."

April blows rings of hot wet air against my chest. "It'll be alright. Daddy." And between the even, smooth, matching teeth she clamps one of the gray hairs and jerking back her head tears it out.

The next morning, an hour before my first class, as I stepped into the shower I noticed the pitpoint cake of blood where the hair had been. During the shower the cake dissolved, revealing the pit open and dark, without a bottom.

Afternoon now. Winter light afternoon. Somewhere, somewhere between Harry's and The Tempo, with a gray hair clutched between her teeth like a flower, April has decided to find herself a young man. Daddies are all right, but young men reflect like windows and brightly polished sports cars. Done, enough.

And let him kick it to death if he can find it.

Winter light afternoon. The slow rain has not stopped, but has frozen into a wall. From my window, from my office high above, I watch students walk through the wall. It seems much easier than it probably is.

"It was just like old times as Ralph Dennis held forth about the writer's life in a back booth at George's Delicatessen...

'I like my life to a certain degree, and I think I chose it. If you chose it, you can't bitch about it 20 years later.'

And whatever he says about his marginal lifestyle, he is not discouraged with the writing career he has chosen.

'I've still got my head about me,' he said. 'I'm going to keep writing till I drop dead. I want to do what I'm doing.'"

—*The Atlanta Constitution*, March 16, 1983

"Ralph Dennis of Atlanta, a writer of paperback mystery novels set in Atlanta, died of kidney failure Monday at Crawford Long Hospital. He was 56. At the time of his death, he was working as an Atlanta bookstore clerk..."

—*The Atlanta Constitution*, July 6, 1988

Printed in Great Britain
by Amazon